"You're driving me crazy..."

Luca gave April a slight tug but it was enough to bring her too close.

He stared at her as if she was made of secrets. "Do you have any idea—" he said, his words so low she might have missed them if she hadn't been just inches away. He opened his mouth once more, only to pull her into a searing kiss.

Oh, God. His lips, warm, urgent, on hers. His arms suddenly wrapped around her, holding her tight. His tongue seeking entry, teasing her to open her mouth.

All coherent thought vanished. It was what she'd wanted since the second night. This kiss, this heat, this urgency between them.

She tasted a hint of wine and something that belonged to Luca. Him. His scent, his hard body pressing against her, his erection growing and pulsing between them.

He wasn't her dream man, he couldn't be, not after all that had happened. She knew better than to believe that fairy tale. But he sure kissed like him.

His guttural moan was so intimate and erotic...and April knew she wasn't going to be the one to say no.

Dear Reader,

Now, here's a real welcome to New York: a long bus trip, stolen savings, breaking and entering (well, not so much breaking), a looming arrest and meeting the hero for the first time in nothing but your bikini panties!

That's April Branagan's first day in the Big Apple.

Lucky for her, she's crash-landed at Luca Paladino's new apartment. Somehow she convinces him to let her stay. Then he can't bear to see her go! But things get complicated when Luca tries a little too hard to help fiercely independent April, and it almost tears them apart. In the end, though, love saves the day. Thank goodness.

I hope you enjoy the second book in my NYC Bachelors miniseries! Look for the final book in the trilogy, madly handsome Dominic's story, coming in April 2017!

Oh, and did I tell you I was in Little Italy last October? After writing this book I'm more than ready to go again. I ❤ NY!

Ciao,

Jo Leigh

Jo Leigh

—

Daring in the City

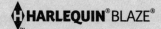

⟨H⟩ HARLEQUIN® BLAZE®

Recycling programs
for this product may
not exist in your area.

ISBN-13: 978-0-373-79949-7

Daring in the City

Printed in U.S.A.

Jo Leigh is from Los Angeles and always thought she'd end up living in Manhattan. So how did she end up in Utah in a tiny town with a terrible internet connection, being bossed around by a houseful of rescued cats and dogs? What the heck, she says, predictability is boring. Jo has written more than forty-five novels for Harlequin. Visit her website at joleigh.com or contact her at joleigh@joleigh.com.

Books by Jo Leigh

Harlequin Blaze

NYC Bachelors

Tempted in the City

It's Trading Men

Choose Me
Have Me
Want Me
Seduce Me
Dare Me
Intrigue Me

To get the inside scoop on Harlequin Blaze and its talented writers, visit Facebook.com/BlazeAuthors.

All backlist available in ebook format.

Visit the Author Profile page at Harlequin.com for more titles.

The Paladino Legacy

IN THIS GENTLY reimagined tale of Little Italy, the Paladino family has lived in their house on Mulberry Street in Little Italy since 1910. When Antonio Paladino, the brothers' great-great-grandfather cobbled together some money working as a skilled mason, the first thing he did with it was buy property.

By the time Joseph Paladino had his three sons, the Paladinos owned a great deal of what is now the very heart of Little Italy. The Paladino Trust had been set up years ago to protect the properties and the family's privacy in the hope of preserving Little Italy. Each of the three sons owns property within the Trust, comprised of both commercial businesses and housing.

But none of the family has any intention to sell. The people in the tight-knit community have no idea that the Paladinos are their landlords, hidden behind the name that had been assigned to the Trust. They believe they have a rent-control situation that keeps their rents reasonable—unlike the rest of the newly gentrified Lower East Side of Manhattan.

1

"WATCH IT!"

Luca followed his brother's gaze across the gutted floor of the Grasso home and let out a breath. "It's okay. She's got it."

"She almost hit Frankie with that beam," Tony said.

"She did not. You're just worried because she's a girl."

"Hey, up yours. You know better than that."

Luca laughed. If his brother didn't know when he was screwing around by now, then that was his problem. Luca had enough of his own.

"Whoa, is that the famous Tony Paladino?" Sal's booming voice came from behind them, and they both turned around. "What's got you in a hard hat, boss? You felt like slumming today, or what?"

"I thought I'd take a break from the office. That okay with you?"

Sal grinned and slapped Tony on the shoulder. "I'm just messing with you. I bet you came by to check up on my niece. The girl's got chops," he said, glancing over at her. "Carlita's still green but she's gonna do a good job."

"I'm not worried," Tony said and ignored Luca's snorting laugh.

"Yeah, I know," Sal said. "I heard that you're too busy looking for wedding rings to bother with remodels."

Luca turned on Tony. "You're looking for rings? Why didn't you say anything?"

Tony took off his hard hat and ran a hand through his hair. "One ring," he said, shaking his head. "I saw a ring in a window and I asked about it. That's it. What I want to know is who's spying on me and shooting off their mouth?"

Luca, along with Sal and several others on the construction crew laughed. As if anyone could get away with anything in their tight-knit neighborhood. Gossip ran like wine through Manhattan's Little Italy and no one was safe.

"Hey, Tony, while I've got you here," Sal said, "I'm going to change the schedule on the Hester Street apartments. We've got two vacancies there so we can go in and take care of the plumbing before they're occupied again."

Tony nodded, and Luca thought about the last time he'd been the subject of gossip—way back during his junior year at Columbia when he'd bought his first motorcycle and rode it home one weekend. Pretty lame as far as gossip went. But when had he had time to get into any real trouble?

What was supposed to have been five years of hitting the books, partying and hooking up—not necessarily in that order—had been interrupted by Tony's rocky marriage, their dad's first heart attack and the damn recession that had slowed construction in the city down to a trickle.

Luca left Tony talking to Sal, the project manager in charge of several of their remodels. After a quick word with Frankie, who was taking measurements for the drywall, Luca thought about his brother ring shopping. It made sense.

After their father's second heart attack, Tony had taken over the company so smoothly there hadn't been a single complaint. Somehow he'd managed to stay on top of his new responsibilities. At the same time, he'd fallen hard for Catherine. They were perfect for each other. Luca could definitely see them getting married soon.

Luca wished his future was a little more certain. At thirty, he'd managed to complete his architecture degree and a year's credit toward his required three-year internship, he had a good job working for the family business and a steady income. He knew he was luckier than most people in every way that counted. But that didn't stop him from feeling somewhat adrift.

His folks were so proud of the idea of his becoming a "big-deal architect" that he couldn't imagine what they would think if they knew what he really wanted to do was focus on his carpentry. And not just the finishing work he did for the business, but the custom pieces he made on the side.

Right now Paladino & Sons had great opportunities doing remodels and renovations all over Lower Manhattan. But with an in-house architect, they could expand into a whole new market—public buildings, chain stores and even military contracts. Jobs that, while they wouldn't offer much creativity, would bring a major increase in cash flow and, more important, steady work for their stable of loyal construction crews.

Presently, Luca had the last two years of his required internship lined up at a prestigious firm, after which he'd be eligible for his professional license. His family was counting on him.

"Hey."

Luca hadn't seen his brother walk up to him. "What's up?"

"That's what I was gonna ask you," Tony said. "You seem distracted. Everything okay?"

"Yeah, sure. Everything's fine. Just, uh… I've asked a couple of guys from the Sanders project to come help me move some stuff to the Mercury Building."

"What stuff?"

"Mostly equipment and tools, but some of my personal stuff, as well. I'm moving into the apartment while I do the renovations."

Tony's eyebrows rose pretty damn high. "Now?"

"Yeah, now. Angelo finished putting in the new pipes, the electrical is done and I've started busting down walls. So I'll live upstairs while I work on the downstairs." In accordance with the Paladino Trust— the one that decreed no one but the immediate family could know that the Paladinos owned a great deal of real estate in the Little Italy area and kept the old timers' rents ridiculously low—Luca had claimed one of the two-story apartments on the top floor of the family-owned building.

Tony shook his head. "What about your internship?"

"The offer's open-ended," Luca said. "It'll still be there when I'm ready."

Tony frowned. "When you're ready? You've been ready for years."

"I didn't mean it like that." Except he kind of did, and that was the problem. Tony knew about his side job. But Luca doubted either of his brothers understood just how much he loved working with his hands. And his parents? Forget about it. They'd short-circuit. Tell him he was wasting his smarts and his education.

The thing was they wouldn't be wrong. Damn, he felt bad about spending all that money for an Ivy League education. He really did. Ironically, it had taken all those years of school to make him realize that being an architect wasn't what he wanted to do with his life.

"You realize I can handle things without you, right? The company won't fold while you step back." Tony bumped his shoulder. "Besides, you know how much government work we're missing out on while we wait for you?"

"Look, I don't want to get into a big discussion about this." Now who couldn't take a joke? He knew Tony was teasing but he'd hit a sore spot. "I can't live with the folks anymore, okay? Now that Dad's home all the time, they're always bickering. It's not even that, though. I haven't lived on my own for a long time. I barely date, because I'm not about to bring a woman back to their place. I'm feeling pressure to get married already, and I just need some room to breathe. I mean, how am I supposed to ever hook up? Keep a room at the Marriott?"

Tony nodded. "Yeah, that's true. You only had, what, two years of living on your own at college? I was all caught up in trying to patch things up with Angie when you moved back home. You really stepped up, man. Took care of the folks. Helped out more than your share with the company."

"Yeah, well, I'm not complaining."

"I know." Tony shook his head. "You seeing anyone now?"

"You mean other than the women Mom and Nonna keep shoving at me?"

"Wait. Are you getting laid at all?"

"Do I look like a guy who's getting laid?" he said, realizing he should've kept his voice down. "That's why I have to get out of there. I have a date next week, one *I* arranged, so hopefully…"

"All right, I see your point. A year after I got divorced they started harassing me about getting married again."

"I remember. And now that you have Catherine they've started going after me. So, yeah, thanks for that."

Tony laughed. "Look, if you want to take some time off to get situated, we'll be fine. I'm ready to get out of the office more so I can step in, and Dom's doing great."

Luca knew his contribution to the company wasn't exactly crucial. The employees and subcontractors they had were top-notch. His brothers could easily carry his load. The only thing that would actually make a difference in their collective future was his becoming licensed.

If only being an architect was what he really wanted.

"And after that," Tony said, "think about taking a step back from the company and pouring yourself into that internship at Willingham. We all had to regroup when Dad got sick, but it's not fair to hold you back when all you've got is two more years of interning before you start your dream career."

Dream career? Luca kept his expression neutral, not wanting to worry his brother. But why the hell couldn't he have figured this stuff out before he'd returned to school?

Deep down he'd probably known then he was on the wrong track. But by that time Tony was in the middle of his divorce and understandably distracted. It had fallen to Luca to take his dad to all his doctors' visits. Interpret what the doctor was saying. His mom had been worried sick and sometimes she got things confused.

Add to that the responsibility of managing the Paladino Trust when so many of their tenants had been hit hard by the downturn in the economy, and his life hadn't been his own. The rest of his family had done what they could but it hadn't been easy.

It certainly wasn't how he'd imagined his college years being. Not that he would do anything different if he had to do it over again. Family was family.

But this was going to be *his* time. He'd act crazy if he wanted. Bring home a different woman every night, although that wasn't like him. The point was the apartment would be all his and he could do whatever he pleased.

Still, the fact remained that everyone was counting on him to get his license and expand the business, but his true passion lay elsewhere.

"I don't mean to tell you what to do," Tony said, his dark brows furrowed. "I'm just—"

"Good. You can stop talking. What part of 'I don't want to get into a big discussion about this' did you not hear?"

"Wiseass." Tony chuckled. "You better be careful. Once you start fixing up your apartment, the match-making will get even worse. And now Pop's on his 'wanting grandkids' kick."

"I know. At least I won't have to listen to them anymore every morning over coffee."

"I get it." Tony nodded. "I don't know what to tell you. It's the fate of all Paladino sons. I heard Nonna has started in on Dominic. Can you imagine?"

"As if he doesn't already have a parade of women knocking at his door."

Tony nodded. "Face it, Luca. You're screwed."

Tony didn't know the half of it.

2

"WES, WHERE ARE YOU?" If only April Branagan had been able to sleep, maybe she wouldn't feel so awful about Wes not calling her back over the last twenty-nine hours. "I'm on the bus. We're pulling out of the station. This is it. I'm really on my way. I know everything's probably fine, but please, whatever you're doing, call me, okay? I want to try to get some rest before I reach Manhattan."

She hung up the phone and made sure she didn't need to plug it into the handy power outlet beside her seat. In fact, this would have been a very enjoyable ride if she hadn't been up for almost two days, and if she'd heard from a certain someone who was supposed to be meeting her at the other end.

The trip from St. Louis to the Port Authority in New York would take over twenty-six hours, with eight stops and a transfer in Chicago. She'd planned to sleep most of the way, but instead, she was a nervous wreck.

To make things worse, the guy sitting across the aisle from her—a thirtysomething travel writer typing on his laptop—kept staring at her legs, which was making her uncomfortable. Until she realized she was jiggling her foot. Probably shaking the whole row.

She stopped. Gave him a conciliatory smile. Heard him hit the keyboard again as she watched her hometown disappear street by street.

By the time they'd gone ten miles, her mind had gone right back to worrying. Where the hell was Wes? Her ex-boyfriend/current business partner had gone ahead to New York to settle their living arrangements and meet up with some college friends who lived in Manhattan and had the connections she and Wes needed to get their fledgling concierge business off the ground.

Their last conversation had been great. He'd been excited about seeing her and showing her the temporary apartment he'd found for them. So why wasn't he picking up?

The guy across the aisle was gathering up his things. One glance told her she was the reason. He stood, taking the time to give her an evil look.

Ah. Her leg was bouncing again. "Sorry," she said, but he didn't respond. At least now she had the row to herself.

Maybe if she just closed her eyes for a bit?

That lasted about two minutes.

Wes had managed to get an amazing deal on a place in Nolita, which, she'd quickly learned, meant the area north of Little Italy, in a building that was being remodeled. It was just a small room and a bathroom on the second floor of an empty apartment, but it was cheap, belonged to a friend of a friend and, well, they didn't need all that much in the way of luxuries. The biggest problem would be the sleeping arrangements.

Wes knew their relationship was and would remain strictly business. They'd actually been over for a while.

April knew he'd hoped the break they'd taken would only be temporary, but she had to wonder if he wasn't answering because he knew her mind was made up and he was pissed about it. Although he'd had plenty of time to tell her he didn't want to move forward with their business plans. She figured there had to be a good reason why he hadn't been in contact, and she couldn't help but worry that he'd been in an accident, or the victim of a mugging—or worse.

She stopped herself. No use sending herself into more of a tizzy. She'd find out what was going on soon enough.

At their stop in Chicago, she ordered a croissant and a large double espresso venti from a kiosk in the bus terminal then added a double-chocolate brownie and a blueberry muffin. She'd probably gain ten pounds before she even got to the most amazing restaurant city in the world.

The transfer to the new bus went smoothly, but it also meant the end of no neighbors. This time a lady wearing a Chicago Bears hat sat in the seat right next to her, pulled out a paperback book, then turned to face April. "I'm Lorene. Lorene Patrick. I'm going all the way to Toledo, and it's my first time there. But I've got a job waiting for me. And my friend, Kiki, she's letting me share her apartment until I can find a place of my own. Where are you headed?"

April stuffed half her muffin into her mouth, just to give her time to adjust to this new situation. Her first thought was to move seats immediately, but then she thought that Lorene might be the distraction she needed.

She was wrong. So very wrong. Lorene ended up talking her ear off for the next three hours before enough people had left the bus that April could finally claim a new seat. The first thing she did was call Wes. Of course he didn't answer. She'd already sent three stealth texts while Lorene had been talking. And talking.

By now April wanted to strangle him. "Goddamn it, Wes. Where are you? Why aren't you answering? Do I really have to call every hospital in New York to make sure you're still alive? You'd better have a damn good excuse for this bullshit. I'm giving you one more hour, and then I'm going to call the police."

The worst thing about cell phones was the inability to smash down a receiver. She made do by punching the disconnect button five times. It didn't help.

April turned toward the window and stared at the lights of South Bend, feeling disembodied. She was so incredibly tired. But closing her eyes just revved her mind up into a spiral of one terrible thought after another.

When her phone actually rang, it made her jump so hard the thankfully quiet woman next to her jumped, too. Fumble-fingered, April finally saw that it wasn't Wes calling. It was her mother.

She pasted a smile on her face, a trick she'd learned working as a waitress. Smiling through terrible situations made them less terrible. And tended to disguise her voice enough that it might earn her a tip. "Hi, Mom."

"I hope I didn't wake you," her mom said. "You hardly got a wink of sleep the last couple of days."

"I'm awake now. Don't worry. I slept all morning. Besides, I should be worrying about you. Did Cassie get all her stuff inside? Are the kids settled yet?"

"It's all coming together. I've put everyone to work, so we'll be done by suppertime. But tell me about your trip. It must be so exciting. Is Wes calling you every twenty minutes?"

"Yeah, sure. Wes is beside himself waiting for me to arrive. He's got the apartment all ready and everything."

Her mother didn't respond right away. "April Michela Branagan, are you telling me the truth?"

"Mom, it's fine. I'm just tired, that's all. Too much excitement, not enough room to burn off my nervous energy."

April glanced at the woman next to her, who didn't even pretend not to be eavesdropping. She turned to the window again and asked her mother to tell her about how the rest of the family was doing.

Her mom and dad had a full house once more. With five kids—only two of them still in school—her folks never did seem to get any peace. Her sister's husband had left her, and Cassie couldn't take care of her kids and afford a place on her salary, so they'd gone where all the Branagan kids seemed to wind up. Back home. God knew where everyone was sleeping. What a mess. Four kids, plus two sets of grandkids meant there was no vacancy at the inn. Which was a little scary for April, considering her business partner wasn't calling her back.

But even if something bad had happened, she wasn't going to let anything get in the way of this plan of theirs. She'd worked too hard, scrimped and saved every dime, to make her dream come true. Whatever was going on with Wes, she'd handle it. She'd make it work. She was good like that. Her dad called her the most determined girl in the whole Midwest. Which was true. Although it was easier to be determined when she wasn't dizzy from not sleeping and she knew what the hell was going on.

"Listen to me, sweetheart," her mom said. "I know how much you want this, and how hard you've worked, but if things don't turn out like you planned, you know you can always come home. New York can be overwhelming. The goal you've set for yourself isn't as simple as finding a job. Don't listen to your father and your brother. Coming home doesn't mean you're a failure. So please promise me that if it gets to be too much, you'll come back."

Tears collected in the corners of her eyes. It *would* be a failure. She believed that with all her heart. She was going to be the first in her family to actually make it. On her own. She'd do whatever it took, no matter what—after she strangled Wes, of course. She'd make it in New York, all right. "Of course, Mom," she said, her voice a little rougher than she would've liked. "I promise."

APRIL STARED UP at the Mercury Building and then at the apartment key in the palm of her hand. Wes had mailed the key to her at the very last minute and she hadn't thought to question it. How could she have been such a fool? Why would she need a key if he had intended to meet her at the bus station?

After she'd arrived at the Port Authority and saw Wes wasn't there waiting for her, she hadn't bothered to call him again. She'd simply slipped on her backpack, collected her heavy rolling suitcase and her enormous nonrolling duffel bag and managed to navigate the subway without bursting into tears.

She double-checked the address to be sure she was at the right place before lugging everything through the building's darkened entranceway, praying the whole time that the key would actually fit the lock of apartment 4A. The first thing she saw was an out-of-order sign taped to the elevator door.

With a small whimper, she started up the stairs. The next problem—she couldn't possibly take both bags at the same time. She'd fall and kill herself before she'd tasted a single slice of real New York pizza.

Making sure no one was watching her, she stashed the duffel in a tight shadowed alcove. She figured it would take her five minutes to get everything else upstairs and then she'd race back to get the bag. It was her only option at this point.

What felt like several hours later, she finally made it to the fourth floor.

Thankfully, the key worked. It was actually someone else's apartment, unoccupied and filled with construction equipment. Soon enough she found the staircase that led to the room Wes had rented.

Her last shred of hope that this was all one great big misunderstanding disappeared when she entered the room.

Of course Wes wasn't there.

She could tell because the room wasn't very large and the closet door was open. There were no clothes in it. None. Zero. In fact, the only things in the room were an unmade mattress with a mess of sheets balled up in the middle, a pillow with no case and a microwave on the window ledge sitting next to a coffeemaker.

Sticking out from beneath the sheets was an envelope with her name printed on it in Wes's handwriting.

Her hand trembled as she slipped out the letter. The black pit of anxiety in her stomach had her feeling nauseated to the point of checking how many steps it was to the bathroom down the hall. At least the toilet seat was up in case she had to make a run for it. She took a deep breath and looked down at the letter.

I'm really sorry. I'll pay you back every penny.
I swear.

The paper floated away as her legs refused to hold her up for another second. She missed the mattress, falling down hard on her knees on the wood floor. It was so much worse than even her nightmare scenarios. He was gone. Actually gone. With her money.

He'd left her in a strange city, in a weird apartment, with a business plan but no partner. He was supposed to handle all the tech. All the research into companies and potential workers. Background checks, safety records. Databases and money exchanges, so they'd bank a piece of every single job they matched. Their business was meant to be like a hotel concierge service complete with guaranteed safety checks.

And he'd disappeared. Ditched her without so much as a warning.

How could he have done this to her? They'd been *lovers*.

Her head dropped into her hands, and there was no holding back the great racking sobs. Not just because he'd stolen her money, but because she couldn't…

God, the expectations of her family had been so important to her, ever since she'd excelled in high school. Before that, really. From a young age, her father had called her The Great Branagan Hope to whoever would listen. He'd laughed, but she knew he'd meant it. The nickname was hauled out with every A, every award, every success she'd earned.

And she'd been brought to her knees on her first day of what was supposed to be her greatest venture yet.

The humiliation was as hard to swallow as the betrayal. She was dizzy by the time she got control of her sobbing. But she hadn't stopped shaking. And it was only then that she remembered she'd left her other bag downstairs.

She took a minute to gain her balance after she stood. When she could walk, she went into the bathroom to wipe her face. Instead of finding a towel, she found toilet paper sitting on the floor. With exactly four sheets left on the roll.

She'd find that son of a bitch, and she'd kill him.

Finally, she started making her way back down the four flights of stairs. It wasn't until she hit the second floor that she noticed a crowd had gathered on the sidewalk.

Two policemen were standing near the broken elevator, their flashlights shining exactly where she'd left her bag. The distorted sounds of their walkie-talkies made her stomach churn.

Hell. She'd been gone too long. They'd found her unattended bag. In New York City. Great. At least there'd be plenty of toilet paper when she was shipped off to Gitmo.

She flew down the stairs. "Wait, wait. That's my bag. I couldn't carry it up with my other giant suitcase and I only meant to leave it for a second but my business partner stranded me and took all my savings. But I swear there's nothing dangerous inside, and I can tell you every single item in there. Just please don't send me to jail."

The two cops stared at her, their hands close to their weapons.

"Honestly," she said, trying to catch her breath, but since her chest was squeezing her lungs flat, it wasn't easy. "My name is April Branagan, but the name tag on the duffel is Eloise Wooster. I borrowed it from my aunt. You can call her if you want, and she'll confirm it. I didn't want to use my name and address because this is a temporary rental, so if it got lost, it could have been lost forever, and it's got all my underwear and a lot of my business clothes.

The good-looking cop put up his hand, stopping her. "Look, we have no choice about this. Any unattended bag left under suspicious circumstances requires a protocol—"

"But it's not suspicious. I swear. I'm standing right here, and if you unzip it even just a tiny bit, I can tell you what you'll find."

"This is a residential building," the shorter cop said. "A lot of people could be at risk."

She looked at him. Then at Hot Cop. Then at all the people who seemed way more interested in the drama than the danger, and she burst into tears. Big, sloppy sobs she had no control over. This was the worst day of her life, and it was becoming more horrifying by the minute.

"You can't tell my mom, okay," she said, crying the words. "I told her I was fine. That I could handle this. She can't afford bail or a flight from St. Louis, not when Cassie's just moved back with her kids."

"Just look in the effin' bag," someone from the crowd said.

She wasn't sure who it was, but it was so nice, it made her cry even harder.

"Yeah, give the girl a break," someone else, a woman, said.

"You think pretty girls can't be terrorists?"

She thought she might throw up. As it was, her nose was running and, of course, she didn't have any tissues with her. "There's an outside pocket," she said, snorting disgustingly. "There are tissues in there, and—" She hiccupped.

Hot Cop said something she couldn't hear to his partner, who pulled up his walkie-talkie, turned away from her and started to speak. She couldn't hear what he said, either, but she figured he was calling the bomb squad and she'd end up at Rikers Island, just like on *Law & Order.*

Then Hot Cop bent next to her bag. He unzipped the side pocket and pulled out the little pack of tissues, showing it to his partner, who nodded.

As she was blowing her nose, which took most of the pack, Hottie unzipped the duffel. He held up the flap so she couldn't see and said, "Tell me what's in here."

"A pink bra and panties, and a white bra and thong, and four more panties—yellow, green, white and lilac— and under that is my kimono robe and then my sleep shirt with the bunnies on it, and the red one with the black lace—"

He pulled out each item, holding them up one at a time to show his partner. And the rest of New York, who seemed to be four deep on the sidewalk, cheering. Hooting. Whistling.

That was when she caught all the phones. Was there even one person who wasn't filming this? With her face looking as if it had gone through a gang initiation and her thong swinging on Hot Stuff's finger?

She sat down on the bottom step of the stairs. Put her head in her hands. All her energy abandoning her in one exhale.

The shorter cop suddenly loomed in front of her. "I still need to file an incident report," he said then glanced back. "Vinny, why don't you clear the area."

Vinny—mercifully taking leave of her duffel bag— stood, gave her a smile that looked a little too much like a leer and then the other officer started firing questions at her. Which was way, way better than the alternative.

3

LUCA DIDN'T GET back to his new place until just after 8:00 p.m. It had turned blustery, and he rubbed his cold hands together as he entered the Mercury Building.

He'd told his folks about his plans. Of course they'd known he was moving out, but they were as surprised as Tony had been about his decision to put off the internship.

Naturally, they'd argued. When did they not argue? But their reaction was what he'd expected. They, like Tony, weren't thrilled, mostly because they'd believed he wanted that architecture license more than he did. Still, two years was a long time to commit to a life that he wasn't certain about.

At the moment, however, his family was the last thing he wanted to think about.

Finally. He had his own place. Tomorrow his bed and wide-screen TV would be delivered, which meant tonight he needed to make sure the path was clear to the stairs. The guys who'd helped him take over the scaffolding and supplies hadn't been choosy about where things landed.

He saw that the elevator was in service again, but he

took the stairs anyway, breathing in the mingled scents of the city and hints of the lives lived down the hallways of each floor. The second and third floors had three apartments each, all occupied. The fourth floor had two exceptional apartments—each of which had two levels.

And now that the annoying Wes was gone, Luca could finally start remodeling—after he got rid of all the guy's shit. At least he'd vacated early. That was the main reason Luca had pushed up his move-in date.

Walking into his new home gave him goose bumps. Maybe it was stupid, but he'd waited a hell of a long time for this moment. It would have been great to stay over tonight, but not without a bed. Tomorrow would be soon enough.

Freedom. Silence. No surprise neighborhood women showing up at dinner. No more playing arbiter among his mother, his father and his grandmother when they got into arguments about what shows to watch on cable. No more questions about where he went at night, who he was with. Was it a girl? Was he being careful?

His first stop, the Sub-Zero fridge he'd had no business installing this soon. All that was left of the old kitchen was the sink and a section of the Formica countertop. He'd have to be careful or risk scratching the stainless steel, but this way he'd have cold beverages while he was working on the place. He'd put a case of beer in there this morning, and he grabbed one now.

After two gulps, he put in his earbuds and tuned his cell phone radio to ESPN, then got down to business putting the tools where they belonged and separating the wood from the drywall.

Hell, the remodel wasn't even going to take that long. Three months max, he decided. He still had to knock down the wall between the master bedroom and the guest room upstairs to give him the space he wanted. But he didn't foresee a problem with that. He figured he could get the place in decent enough shape before his date next week. It didn't have to be perfect.

He'd met Jillian at Columbia when they'd both been studying architecture. She was currently serving her internship so she was used to the different phases of construction.

Tomorrow, after he got rid of Wes's crap, he'd make a decision about the wall. And then he'd bring over some clothes and other personal stuff.

His stomach grumbled, reminding him he hadn't eaten since lunch. Removing his earbuds, he placed a call for a large pepperoni to be delivered. Having a slice and drinking a beer felt like a christening of sorts. Getting laid would've made the inauguration perfect. He hoped next week panned out. He got itchy just thinking about it.

Ten minutes later he thought he heard the buzzer, but no way the pizza was there that fast. He yanked out his earbuds again, and just as he figured he'd been imagining things, a scream tore into his bubble like a gunshot.

He didn't even think, just grabbed the crowbar sitting on a pile of rags, his heart racing. It occurred to him that the scream didn't sound like a help-I'm-being-assaulted scream. Although his only experience as far as that went came from TV or movies.

He moved closer to the door. Another scream, this time louder.

Shit. It was coming from inside his apartment.

Luca glanced up the stairs. Goddamn Wes Holland hadn't moved out. Or he had, but he'd left a woman behind.

Not taking any chances on what he might find, and

cursing himself for doing his friend a favor by letting his buddy move in, he started up the staircase. As he moved stealthily down the hallway he heard her shouting, but he couldn't make out many of the words. "Fucker" came in the clearest, followed by "bastard" and "shithead."

The closer he got to the door, the more words he could understand, but none that explained what was actually going on. He also didn't hear anyone shouting back.

He waited at the edge of the door, finally able to make out all of what she was saying.

"How the hell does promising to pay me back do me any good? Am I supposed to believe you, after this?"

The tears and desperation came through loud and clear.

"That was almost all of my savings. I've worked for years for that money, and you know it," she said. "I hate you so much right now. You're such a coward, you won't even pick up. I'm so disappointed. I hope you're happy, destroying me like this. Were you laughing at me the whole time?"

Luca assumed the woman was talking about Wes and leaving him a voice mail. Had he really run off with her money? For her sake, Luca hoped not, but it wasn't his problem.

Leaning to his left, he risked peeking inside the room. Luckily, the woman had her back to him. Lucky for him because it was a very nice view: the woman was wearing nothing but underwear.

Very tiny underwear.

Her bikini panties were pale blue, resting high on each cheek, and tucked in between her stunning buttocks just far enough to make him catch his breath. On top, he spotted the straps of her matching bra poking out from underneath a cascade of thick auburn hair.

He wondered what she looked like from the front...

She turned quickly, probably hearing his irregular breathing.

Now her scream was definitely of the help-I'm-being-assaulted variety.

He lowered the crowbar, noticing the two large pieces of luggage behind her. "Hey, hey," he said softly, raising his left hand. "I'm not going to hurt you."

She waved her cell phone at him as she grabbed the nearest thing at hand—a pillow—and held it up against her seminaked body. "I've already hit my panic button. The police will be here any minute."

"Good," he said, leaning his weapon against the door frame, trying hard to ignore the fact that she was hot. Certainly way too hot for that douche bag, Wes. "I'm anxious to hear you explain what you're doing in my apartment."

"Your apartment? You mean you own the one below?"

He nodded. "It's all one unit."

"But I have a key. And five days left on the rental agreement."

"What agreement?"

"My..." Her pause was notable, mostly for the look of fury that passed across her face. "My ex-jerkface business partner rented this place from the—from you, I guess. But I didn't think you lived here."

"Huh. Well, I think you might have been misinformed by Jerkface. And by Jerkface, I'm assuming you mean Wes Holland?"

Her whole demeanor changed from fierce guardedness to utter defeat and she lowered her cell phone. "Wait a minute. How do I know you're the real owner?"

"Wes moved out. Letting him stay here was a favor, one that he didn't value very highly. All this crap was supposed to be gone when he left."

Maneuvering the pillow to cover whatever she could of herself, she grabbed her backpack and pulled out a folded piece of paper. "Ha. You're wrong. This is the rental agreement. Right here." She held it up and wagged it at him, the same way she'd done with her phone.

The truth was, he'd agreed to let the guy stay, and he had moved out early, but there'd been nothing in writing. "Hey, I'm sorry about your friend, but you can't stay here. I'm moving in and working on the apartment. The only reason I rented to him at all was because I hadn't gotten started on the renovation yet. And he never mentioned you."

"But he left a note," she said, her voice wobbling. "He was supposed to meet me at the Port Authority. Help me move in. But he hasn't answered any of my phone calls for two days. And he emptied our joint bank account that was intended for our new business."

Yep, two days ago—that was when Wes had moved out. Luca felt bad for her, but it still wasn't his problem. His gut had told him the guy was a prick. Why the hell hadn't he listened?

"I understand you must be angry," he said, "but that doesn't change the fact that you'll have to leave."

"What? Now?"

"Well, no." It was already late, well past dark, and he couldn't see himself throwing her out. "You can stay tonight, but you'll have to go tomorrow."

A couple of very white teeth tugged on her lower lip. "Look, if you could just let me stay for the next five days? By then I'll have found somewhere else. I'll have figured out what to do."

"May I suggest you get on the next Greyhound back to wherever you came from?"

A single tear trickled down her cheek and she quickly turned away. "I can't. There's no place for me there. I've planned this move for a while. We had everything set up to start our business…" Her voice trailed off, ending in a muffled sob. "Fine, I'll go," she whispered. "It can't be in the morning, though. I need to find a place."

He turned to leave, but hesitated at the door while he thought about her predicament. Letting her stay a couple days would mean he'd have to put off moving in upstairs, but it wouldn't put the reno back much. It would just be less convenient for him. But he wasn't a jerkface, and he doubted this was some sort of con.

Technically, he owed her nothing. Luca had agreed to let Wes have the room, not her. But she was in a hell of a spot. Still, what did he know about her?

He waited for her to face him again, and when she didn't he asked, "What's your name?"

"April."

"Is that your real name?"

That got her to turn around. She pinned him with a glare as she wiped her tears as quickly as she could. "Yes. April Branagan. Check me out. I'm not a criminal." Her bravado faltered and she let out a soft whimper. "Although your neighbors might think I am."

"My neighbors?" The hair on the back of his neck stood up. "Why?"

"I didn't say I *was* a criminal. Just that they might think so."

"Why would they think that?" More to the point, why

was he bothering to ask? He should be kicking her cute little behind out the front door right now.

"It was a misunderstanding. That's all. There was no reason to call the cops."

"Cops? Here?"

"No, not up here. Outside." She sniffed and dabbed at her cheek. "And only because the elevator was out of order."

Luca was pretty sure the cops didn't give a rat's ass about the elevator, so he waited, staring at her as she stared back. The pillow slipped a few inches. Either she hadn't noticed or it was a ploy to distract him, which…

Goddamn it.

Her breasts were high and looked firm. He only saw the tops plumping over her pale blue bra. Nothing else was showing. Still, he moved his gaze to safer ground.

If there was such a thing.

He hated to think he'd end up being an idiot because she was hot. Those big dark eyes weren't even the most remarkable thing about her face. It was the odd combination of her roundish cheeks and delicate chin. Or maybe the contrast between her dark brows and warm, rosy skin…

Whatever, she was gorgeous, and his opinion of Wes Holland went down several more notches. The guy was an idiot.

"Tell me why the cops were here," he said, holding up a hand when she started to speak. "In one sentence, and make it good if you want to stay."

She inhaled deeply, and he had to force himself to keep looking at her face. "Because the elevator was out of service and you can see how big my luggage is, I couldn't carry both bags up the stairs at the same time by myself so I stuffed my duffel bag in the alcove by the elevator then I came up here only to find the note that told me Wes had run off with my money, and because of that it took me longer than I'd expected to go back for my duffel, and by that time there were cops downstairs because the bag was unattended, so I had to convince them that I wasn't a terrorist even though the tag on the bag was in my aunt's name, but then they looked inside and found nothing but my clothes so they didn't arrest me, thank God. And that's it. That's why the cops were here."

It was a good thing she'd stopped to take a breath because her face had started turning pink from speed talking her way through that entire monologue. "All right," he said, holding back a laugh. "You can stay. Two days. And everything goes with you."

"Really?"

He nodded, grudgingly. At least he wouldn't feel like a snake.

"You haven't told me your name," she said.

"Luca Paladino."

Hugging the pillow, she held out her hand, and when he took it, he was reminded quite viscerally of how petite she was. Five-one at the most?

"You know, I'm tearing this whole place up. There's going to be a lot of noise and I can't guarantee you'll have electricity."

"I'll deal with it. Thanks." She looked down and quietly muttered, "Even though the rental agreement was for five more days."

He took a step back into the room. "Why don't you let me take a look at that agreement?"

She hesitated, then handed him paper.

The bastard had clearly downloaded a standard rental agreement from the internet and forged Luca's signature. "Be aware that I'm staying downstairs, so keep the screaming to a minimum," he said.

Her shoulders drooped, but she kept her back upright, and her reddened eyes met his gaze straight on. She knew how to school her reactions. Interesting. So maybe she was involved in some kind of con. God, he hoped not. He wanted to believe she was exactly who she purported to be: a victim of a relationship gone bad.

April studied him for several moments then said, "Thank you. You're very kind."

"Just don't make me the schmuck who bought a bunch of your bullshit, okay?"

Quickly wiping one finger underneath her right eye, she shook her head. "I won't. I know far too well what that feels like. But I do have one favor to ask you."

His stomach sank. "Don't you mean another favor?"

She blinked. "Yes," she said, nodding. "Could I borrow a roll of toilet paper?"

"Are you kidding?"

She waved in the direction of the bathroom. "He left me four sheets. Generous, isn't he? Bastard."

"That's got to be a record low." It occurred to him that she could've easily taken a roll from the downstairs bathroom. Instead she'd asked. "Yeah, sure. I'll get it for you."

She tried to give him a smile, but it didn't stick.

On his way down the stairs he played devil's advocate. It was quite possible the toilet paper situation had tipped the scales. Hell, two days was generous, considering he wanted to get a jump on the—

Ah, shit.

He'd almost forgotten about his date. With the very gorgeous and—he was quite sure of it—willing Jillian whom he'd run into at a gallery retrospective. Their date was in seven days. So yeah, April putting him behind schedule was inconvenient. Her being there wouldn't stop him from working on the living room area, but he needed to have access to the upstairs bedroom. Two less days to get it in shape meant he'd have to hustle.

After finding a roll of toilet paper in the old vanity cabinet in the bathroom he was going to tear out, he went back to the staircase.

April appeared above him, dressed in a pair of jeans and a pink T-shirt. She was still hot.

He tossed the roll up, and she caught it handily. "Look, I've got a pizza coming any second. And some beer in the fridge. You're welcome to have some."

Even from this distance he could see she was tempted, but she hesitated. He supposed that was a good sign. Smart. She didn't know him, either.

When she didn't respond, he shrugged. "Suit yourself. But it's a large pepperoni, and the beer is cold."

He turned, leaving her to figure it out. It made no difference to him if she came downstairs. Then it occurred to him that he probably shouldn't go back to his folks' house tonight and leave her here on her own. But then where would he sleep?

Oh, for God's sake, the woman was already too much trouble.

4

EVEN AFTER LUCA had disappeared, April just stood there, not sure she'd be able to move. The thought of going downstairs was more than she could bear. Not the thought of eating with Luca. Just making her way down there.

Instead, she returned to the Wes Abandonment Suite and stared at a spot on the floor. A pain in her shoulder knocked her out of her trance, which was a pity. For a while there, she'd had no thoughts, at least none she could remember. But somewhere in that void, she'd made a decision that surprised her.

She emptied more of her duffel bag until she got to her makeup and facial cleanser. She'd packed a couple of washcloths, mostly because she didn't trust Wes to pick up anything but the cheapest crap.

If only she'd had the foresight to realize that was the least of her concerns.

She really had to let it go, for now at least. She took her things to the bathroom, which was so outdated it looked like something out of a 1950s movie. The toilet was in okay shape, just hard-water stained, as was the area around the sink's drain. The shower looked reasonably clean and there was enough space on the boxy vanity-sink combo for her toiletries. Now all she needed was water.

Wetting her cloth, she put it over her face, concentrating on her puffy, red eyes. The end result, after applying the cool cloth four times, was that she looked as if she had a wicked cold. At least she didn't appear to be on death's door, so that was an improvement.

After brushing her hair, she dabbed a little blush on her cheeks then went to face her next big hurdle.

Luca was standing in the kitchen, a large pizza box balanced on an ugly Formica countertop. He looked up, immediately meeting her gaze, although she hadn't made a sound. When she reached him, he got a beer out of the fridge.

After uncapping the bottle he handed it to her along with a paper towel.

"Thanks." April managed a smile. Completely drained of energy, she felt so weird she couldn't describe it. Nothing seemed real. Not even the long bus ride yesterday— or was that today?

God. Everything was a surreal blur.

"Sorry. No plates."

"That's fine," she said and decided looking into his intense dark eyes was a bad idea. She turned to the shiny stainless-steel refrigerator that didn't belong. At all. "Is that real?"

He followed her gaze, just stared for a moment, before looking at her. Even with a confused expression, he was still smoking hot. "Are we talking about the fridge?"

"Yeah, um… No." Okay. Proof she should've stayed upstairs. "No, we aren't," she said, clearing her throat. "It just looks—" She took a big bite of her pizza to keep her mouth busy. Exhaustion combined with a really attractive guy was not a good mix. Had he been this gorgeous upstairs?

Luca was tall, at least a foot taller than she was, his hair dark brown and silky. He wore it on the long side, pushed back. With his Mediterranean skin tone and last name, she guessed his family was from an Italian coastal town. Naples, maybe? His eyes were dark, his brows full, his jaw strong…but the individual parts weren't as impressive as the whole.

Shit, she was still staring at him.

"You mean the fridge looks too fancy for the Formica?" he asked.

"Yes?"

A faint smile tugged at his mouth.

She took a sip of beer. "So, this place is huge. I thought every apartment in New York was closet-sized."

"A lot of them are. I think the place looks bigger since I took down two walls. It's going to be a nice open space when it's all finished."

"Wow. A two-story apartment. Is that common here?"

"No. I lucked out. I'll be turning half of the upstairs into a screened-in porch. The rest will be my master suite. The porch side is blocked off, so don't go wandering around. It's not safe."

"I won't. I'll just stick to my little ol' room. I should probably get a cooler or something, though," she said, glancing around at the ladders and stacked drywall. "What did Jerkface use? Do you know?"

"Not my brand-new refrigerator."

"I didn't think so." She studied the high-end appliance some more. "That sucker is big. You can't have much in there."

"What are you getting at?" Luca folded his arms across his chest.

A very nice chest to go with his broad shoulders. And muscular forearms. She met his gaze. "Oh, nothing. Just making an observation."

"Right."

"Obviously this is the kitchen," she said, ignoring his skeptical tone. "What are you going to do with the rest of this area?"

"Dining room, living room." He nodded at the wide space between them and the windows then gestured to the right, past the staircase. "Powder room and an office."

"Holy cow. It's going to be gorgeous. You're doing all the work yourself?"

"No. I'll have help, but I'll be doing most of it. My family owns a construction company, so it's pretty much what I do."

April nodded. Yep, that explained the muscular arms. She glanced around, imagining what she'd do with so much space as she finished her slice of pizza, which tasted amazing even though it wasn't that hot anymore. The beer went down great with it, too. "I hope it turns out exactly the way you imagine it will."

He seemed surprised, but she meant it. If there was one thing she understood it was that shit happened, even if a person planned everything down to the tiniest detail.

"Another piece?"

"Oh, I'm not leaving this crust," she said, feeling slightly buzzed. "I'd heard about New York pizza and wondered if it was just a lot of hype. But, wow. For a while there, I thought I was going to be hauled off to jail without ever having a slice. I would've been really pissed."

His smile made her chest warm. For all the grief she'd given him, he was being very hospitable. She sure wished he had chairs, though. Her legs were feeling wobbly again.

Leaning against the island, she took in the old white porcelain sink, what was left of the Formica counter and the fridge. It was really something, not a brand she recognized. Too big for one person, unless that person wanted to share. "You don't have a microwave."

"I will eventually."

"The microwave Wes bought is probably a cheapo but you're welcome to use it."

"Thanks," he said and tipped the bottle to his mouth.

She watched him drain his beer, as fascinated by the working of his jaw and throat as by her sudden instinct to touch him. Dragging her gaze away, she took another hasty sip of her own beer and found the bottle was empty. That might be for the best. The point of her visit hadn't been to get buzzed or to sponge food off her landlord. She'd just wanted to make nice. And maybe do a little negotiating. She needed him to let her stay just a little bit longer, until she got settled and recovered from the shock of this scary predicament.

"I just want you to know how much I appreciate this," she said. "You're being really nice about everything, and well, before I go I just…"

The way his eyes narrowed made her rethink her approach.

"I think I would like another slice."

He set her up with seconds of both pizza and beer and grabbed another bottle for himself. As she bit into her slice, she walked over to the large window that looked out onto Mott Street. "Café Roma?" she said. "Is that a good place for Italian food?"

"Yeah. It is."

She looked back at him. "Since I'm in Little Italy I want to try something I wouldn't find in St. Louis." She'd thought he might offer some suggestions, but he stayed quiet. "It's a very busy street, but I'm not hearing any traffic."

"Special windows."

"Triple glazed?"

He nodded, and once again it appeared that she'd surprised him. "It won't keep out sirens, but for regular traffic, it works great."

She took another pull of her beer, which made her feel a tiny bit dizzy. Maybe this would go better if she sat down. Looking around, she saw a big wooden shipping crate, which, according to the label, was filled with wine, a stepstool that she could have perched on except it was awfully close to the floor and a stack of boards. None of the options appeared very stable, and she figured she probably shouldn't overstay her welcome, anyway. Which meant she needed to get on with things.

"Could you be a bit more specific about exactly how long I'm allowed to stay?" she blurted.

Luca's eyes closed for a second.

"I'm just asking because, well, today really doesn't count, what with me getting here so late. It would have been impossible for me to look for housing tonight, so what do you say we count tomorrow as day one? That will give me more of a chance to do some research and make some calls. That is, if there's a place nearby where they serve cheap coffee and have free Wi-Fi?"

"Wait a minute—"

"I mean, all that was supposed to have been done by

Wes. He was in charge of finding a permanent place for us to live. I have no idea where he looked, or if he even looked at all. And yes, I know it's not your problem but I don't have anyone to call or to give me tips or even a couch to sleep on."

"April—"

"I'm not trying to get anything more out of you, honest."

His lips pressed together, but he didn't tell her to take a flying leap.

"Unless, I can?"

His deepening scowl said she was pressing her luck.

"But, no. You've been so nice already, and I don't want to take advantage of you. Although, there is just one more little thing… Since Wes had paid for the next five days there should be a small refund, right?"

"He didn't."

"What?"

"He left without paying for the last week he was supposed to stay here. Which is why I figured he was gone for good."

She sagged. But she would mope later. Instead, stopping to consider that she was lucky, under the circumstances, she pulled out a commiserating smile. "I'm very sorry he did that to you," she said. Then a very unpleasant thought occurred to her. "That means I owe you for the two days."

Frowning, Luca set down his beer. "No, you don't."

"Yes, I do. So, let's see… Two days would mean…" She rubbed her temple, trying hard to do the math. "I'm usually good with numbers. I guess I'm just too tired. Would you mind doing the calculation and letting me know what I owe?"

"Look, April—"

"I won't stay for free." Before she even realized something was wrong, she had to brace her hand on the wood cabinet to keep from falling over. The dizziness passed as quickly as it had come. She guessed hearing yet another bad thing about Wes had made her head spin.

"You all right?"

"Yeah, sure."

Luca cleared his throat, picked up a tarp that had been folded neatly on top of a tool chest and draped it over the case of wine. "Travel days are the worst," he said. "Especially by Greyhound." He gestured for her to sit down.

She stumbled a little before she planted her butt on the makeshift seat. "No, it was okay. The problem wasn't the bus, it was the lack of sleep even before I boarded, then not hearing from the jackass, then the elevator situation, then me almost going to prison and now you wanting to throw me out."

He coughed, and she realized what she'd said.

She blinked up at Luca, who was watching her with a hint of a smile and an arched right eyebrow. Instead of questioning that look, she yawned. A real jawbreaker. Which let loose a wave of exhaustion that hit her like a tidal wave. "I really should go get some sleep."

"I agree. I don't think the beer helped, either."

"No, it probably didn't. I'm not much of a drinker, and I rarely have beer, although this one was really good."

"Look, even knowing I should have my head examined, I'm going to let you manipulate me into that extra day."

"Thank you. That's very nice." April really needed to get upstairs. Her head kept getting fuzzier. "So, I'll plan on leaving the morning after the second night. Not counting tonight."

With another shake of his head, he said, "What is it you did in St. Louis?"

"Hmm? Oh, lots of jobs. During and after college I worked everything from construction to pet sitting to serving promotional drinks to drunk businessmen. That one was the most lucrative, although getting my ass pinched got old real quick."

"So, you never worked in sales, huh? You know, you look as though you're about to fade away. Why don't you let me walk you to your room?"

She laughed. "It's just upstairs."

"The last thing we need is you falling and breaking something."

"Not to mention suing you. I wouldn't do that. Wes, on the other hand, would. Can you believe him? How could I not have realized he was an epic asshole? That's very disturbing. I'm going to have to think about that one—" She yawned. "Just not tonight."

Luca stood close, and looking up at him made the room spin. She took another sip of her beer, belatedly remembering it was ill-advised.

"Wait a minute. Don't move," he said. A moment later he was back, holding a bottle of water. Then he put a hand on her back and helped her stand. Which was very nice of him. So was his sliding an arm around her waist and pulling her against him.

He was so much bigger than Wes. Taller, stronger, more muscular. He smelled good, too. Masculine. She was pretty sure he wasn't wearing any cologne, either, at least not the kind Wes stocked up on. "He liked to smell like the woods," she said. "Wes, I mean. But he hated the woods. Hated camping. Made me take care of all the spiders."

"Did he?"

As they got closer to the stairs she found herself leaning more heavily against Luca. "You're nice, though. Thank you for this. For letting me stay. I'll be out of your hair before you know it."

"I'm sure of it. Come on now, step up. We can do this."

It took some concentration for her to climb up the staircase. Or maybe she was simply distracted by the man who was helping her. His body felt warm and solid. His arm tightening around her made her feel safe. So foolish. She didn't know him. She just needed to get him to let her stay until she could find a job—heck, several jobs—so she could earn enough to find a place to live that wasn't a cardboard box.

"No way I'm not going to start my own business," she said as they made it to the second-floor landing. "No way that asshat's going to stop me."

"Good for you," he said, walking her to the bedroom door. "Here, take this." He handed her the water.

It took a moment for her to get a grip on it, as she was busy feeling bereft again. About Wes. About the loss of Luca's arm around her waist. About the stupid mattress and wrinkled sheets. She looked up at him one more time, steadying herself with a hand on his very broad, hard chest. "I'll pay you back, you know. For the pizza and beer. And water. For the next two nights. I pay my way," she said. "No matter what."

"Okay, we can talk about that tomorrow. For now, though, I think you should get some sleep, huh?"

She slid her palm off his chest and listed to the left. His arms came all the way around her, and she leaned gratefully against his chest, so tired and weak she didn't know how she was going to make it to the mattress. When she fully realized what she was doing, she straightened away from him. "Sorry," she muttered.

"It's okay. You're crashing from all that adrenaline from earlier." He loosened his arms but didn't pull away. "Take your time."

"You're a nice man, you know that?"

Luca smiled. "Yeah, I'm a real peach."

"You are." April smiled back at him as he turned her toward the room. "I'll vouch for you."

"You don't know me. I could be a real scumbag."

"No, you're not," she said as he gave her a gentle push forward. "I just know it."

"You thought you knew Wes," Luca reminded her.

Her stomach clenched, and she stumbled into the room and waited until he shut the door behind him before the tears fell.

5

UPON REFLECTION, LUCA realized he'd been an idiot. And because he didn't like doing things half-assed, he'd gone for the gold. Yep, he'd attained a whole new level of stupidity.

Yawning, he sat up and rubbed his eyes. He really could have slept at his folks' house last night, instead of on a pile of tarps. He hadn't heard a peep out of April since they'd parted ways last night, and even if she had decided that she would rob him blind, what could she have taken? Drywall? Ladders? But she was in a strange house, in a strange city, and he hadn't wanted to leave her alone.

Although the truth was April needed to learn very quickly that she shouldn't be so trusting of strangers. Not in New York City.

Hell, he should be taking his own advice. He didn't know her. She was already complicating his life. And she'd caused him actual, physical pain. Indirectly, but still. With a muffled groan he got to his feet and stretched. He didn't even have the comfort of coffee to make him feel better.

In a minute he'd run over to the corner bodega for

some strong Colombian and pick up a few toiletries at the same time.

Luca dragged his palm down his stubbled jaw. This was ridiculous. He wasn't thinking clearly. There was no point in coming back here until later in the day. He might as well go straight to his folks' house and pack the last of his things.

He saw his shirt hanging on the ladder where he'd left it, but where was his phone? He checked his jeans' pocket then saw it lying next to the pizza box. Of course he had messages. The first one stopped him.

"Dammit."

His bed and wide-screen delivery. They were coming in an hour.

Shit, shit, shit.

He was supposed to have called the store last night to push the date back. Then April had come downstairs, and his mind had gone down a road that was strictly off-limits. So what had he done? Fed her. Got her tipsy. Helped her to bed.

At least he hadn't crawled in with her. For a minute there, when she'd leaned into him, he'd had a devil of a time letting go of her. Just thinking about it was re-awakening his morning wood, and he made a dash for the bathroom. The delivery guys were coming soon. Normally he could count on them being late. But with his luck, traffic would be so light they would set some kind of record.

He had to be ready for when they got there. There was only one place he could put his bed now that she was using the room upstairs. The office wasn't large enough to hold more than just the king-size bed and a few boxes, and it had no door, but it would have to do. Of course, he'd have to use a couple guys to help him get the bed upstairs after April left, but he couldn't worry about that now. The pathway to the office was blocked by yesterday's efforts to organize his work space. Perfect.

Sans caffeine, every muscle and joint in his body aching, he got to work. Starting with a stack of beams, he lifted as many as he could without making him actually cry, and took them all the way to the far wall. Next, he had to move the drywall. Unfortunately, he'd stacked a ton of it in the office, but there was nothing he could do but carry the heavy mothers two at a time out into the living room.

"Hello?"

April. Just what he needed. She stood at the bottom of the staircase, looking well rested and pretty. Damn her. Her hair was in a ponytail, her bangs pushed to the side, and she was wearing skinny jeans and a T-shirt that was at least one size too small for his comfort.

"Can I help you carry that?"

He thought about it. But no, she needed to get a jump on looking for someplace else to live and stop complicating his life. "No, that's okay," he said, starting a stack of drywall next to the front windows before heading back to the office to get more.

"Um, okay, but I'm pretty strong," she said, following him. "And not that I want to interrupt your work or anything, but I was wondering if you could tell me how much I owe you for the nights I'll be staying here? And where I can find an ATM close by?"

Huh. He hadn't expected her to be so persistent and he had no idea what to charge her. He picked up two sheets then turned to face her. She'd been staring at his back but quickly met his gaze. She was young, healthy, and while she probably couldn't lift a seventy-pound sheet, she could carry boxes and paint cans and tools.

"Tell you what," he said, glancing at his watch. "You help me move the smaller stuff to the front of the apartment, and I'll let you stay for nothing."

Her eyes widened. "Seriously?"

"That's the offer."

"Okay, yeah." She glanced at the drywall and then lowered her gaze, her cheeks turning pink. Probably embarrassed about last night, though she didn't need to be. "I can help move those, too."

"They're heavy."

She nodded. "Don't worry about it. I've worked with my dad on lots of building projects. I'm stronger than I look."

"Okay, but for now, grab that paint can and follow me."

They made the short trip in silence, with him leading the way. Damn, he was tempted to send her on a coffee run. But they didn't have much time, so they walked back to the office, and he let her lift the next panel, but he could see her struggling.

"I think we'll get more done if we do two at a time, together."

"You can handle two by yourself so that doesn't make sense," she said, still having difficulty meeting his eyes. "It's not the weight giving me trouble, it's because I'm short. Let's try three at a time."

Luca hesitated. "If it's too heavy you let me know."

"Okay," she said, her eagerness disconcerting. He wondered if this trade had been a mistake, but he didn't give a damn. Not when he felt this shitty.

The plan worked. For such a little thing, she had some muscle. And she didn't complain, even though he could tell it wasn't easy for her. Quicker than he could have done by himself, they'd cleared out the room.

When the last paint can was gone, he needed a breather, but even more than that, he needed coffee. "Here's an idea," he said, pulling out his wallet. "There's a café several doors down. How about picking us up two large coffees?"

"Oh, God, yes. But I'll buy. Anything else?"

He shook his head, concerned that she still couldn't look him in the eye. "I'm having some things delivered shortly. After that, I'll think about breakfast. You go ahead, though."

She nodded and hurried to the door as he put his wallet away.

"April?"

Her hand on the doorknob, she turned and smiled, and predictably her gaze lowered.

"You don't need to be embarrassed about last night."

"I know," she said, sighing. "But I am a little bit. Even one beer in my condition was stupid. You were great, though, so thanks."

"No problem."

She opened the door and hesitated. "I forgot to ask… sugar, cream?"

"Just black."

"Got it." She cleared her throat, about to say something else.

Luca braced himself. He'd given her an opening by offering a trade and now he was about to regret it.

April just smiled again and slipped out the door.

Now he was curious. But he couldn't stand around thinking about how good she looked from behind when his stuff would be arriving any minute.

Luca moved the tarps near the unassembled scaffolding then manhandled the wine crate and set it by the living room cable outlet. He put a sturdy piece of wood on top of the crate so his wide-screen TV would rest safely in front of his—

The recliner…

"Shit."

Charlie had mentioned that he and his crew could pick it up from Luca's folks' house and drop the recliner off with the rest of the tools and equipment he needed. That didn't necessarily mean today. Luca was fairly certain his brother had Charlie's crew working in Queens.

Before he could start clearing the way for the chair—just in case—a pair of delivery guys arrived with his new bed and TV. As he suspected, the bed just fit, leaving him very little room to maneuver.

While the men went back down to get the wide-screen, Luca finished making room for the recliner. He wasn't crazy about the idea of working anywhere near the TV, but it was only for a couple of days. He was relatively sure he wouldn't destroy it.

He'd left the front door open for the delivery guys and heard Charlie's booming laughter coming from down the corridor. Of course he'd chosen to come by today. Jesus. Luca shook his head. Again, one phone call could've solved the problem.

"Hey, what's up?" Charlie said as he walked in, glancing around. "You're getting serious about this remodel."

Scott and Elliot followed behind him with an electric sander and a ton of drop cloths. Great, more things Luca didn't have room for at the moment. All three men stared at him, and then Charlie grinned and whistled.

Luca turned sharply toward the door. He figured it was April. Nope. They were grinning at him. "What?"

"Show-off," Charlie said. "Must be nice having time for the gym."

"The gym? Yeah, right. I haven't been there in—" Shit. He glanced down at his bare chest then looked at the ladder where he'd hung his shirt. It wasn't there, but he found it on the floor.

Jesus. He'd been working the whole time shirtless. With April. But she hadn't said a word.

"Where do you want us to put your recliner?" Scott asked. "It's on the truck."

Luca was tempted to make them take it back to his parents' house. For not calling first. And for whistling. He scooped up the shirt and just as he was about to pull it on he noticed April. She stood in the doorway, looking uncertain.

"You can set it over here," Luca told Scott, nodding at the spot where he'd slept. Then he motioned for April to join them.

The three guys, all of them in their twenties and notorious horndogs, eyed her, then him, then her again.

He pulled on his shirt, knowing without a single doubt that April hadn't been avoiding his eyes this morning. She'd been wondering why the hell he was walking around half-naked.

She came up to him with a soft smile and waited for him to finish buttoning his shirt before she held out his coffee.

"Thanks," he muttered and turned a glare on the three mutts who continued to stare at her. "You guys must not be busy today."

"What?" Charlie glanced at him and then looked at the other two. "Hey, go get the recliner. And don't forget the two boxes."

"Boxes? I didn't ask you to bring any boxes."

"I know," Charlie said, shrugging. "I tried telling those two lunkheads…" He smiled at April. "Hey."

"Hello." She smiled. "I'm April."

Charlie glanced at her extended hand, wiped his palm on his jeans and then shook it as if he was afraid he'd break her. "I'm Charlie."

Luca sighed. "I work with these guys."

"Where do you want this TV?" It was the kid from the department store backing into the room.

"Over here." Luca kicked some rags out of the way.

April set down her cup and started helping.

"Go ahead, drink your coffee. We can rearrange things later." Aware of how that might've sounded, he didn't dare look at Charlie. "Let's just get out of their way for now."

"Should I go upstairs?" she whispered.

"Only if you want to. They shouldn't be long."

While they drank their coffee, the guys brought up the recliner and the two boxes. It didn't take long. The TV worked. He was glad for the recliner, after all, and even more glad for the boxes once he remembered what he'd thrown in one of them. Brand-new toiletries he hadn't even opened yet.

He signed for the bed and wide-screen TV, and tipped the two delivery guys.

Charlie stood off to the side, sneaking looks at April. Scott and Elliot were doing the same thing while they folded the protective pad they'd used for the recliner. Only they were much better at disguising it than Charlie.

"Okay, boss, is that it?" Scott asked, and almost before Luca answered, he and Elliot both had their hands out.

Luca snorted. "You want a tip? Get back to your real

jobs before my brother strangles all of us." He laughed along with them as they walked to the door. "Wait," he said, digging into his pocket. "I want to buy your lunch."

"No," Charlie and Elliot said at the same time. "No way."

"Hell, we were just kidding," Scott said. "We're not taking your money. You'd do the same for us."

"Nah, I wouldn't." Luca tried to slip a bill to Charlie, but they all headed for the door. "I hate to tell you guys, I have an ulterior motive. In a few days I'll need you to help me haul everything upstairs. Including the king bed."

He felt April tense beside him.

"No sweat," Charlie said. "Nice meeting you, April."

The three of them were heading down the corridor when Luca heard Scott say, "Hey, how do you know her name?"

Sighing, Luca rubbed the back of his neck. All he wanted was to go crash on his new bed, but he couldn't. He'd taken today off for a reason, and he couldn't afford to sleep away the time.

The hand on his arm almost made him drop his coffee. It sent a shiver down his spine, and the urge to touch her back was stronger than it had any right to be.

"I honestly didn't understand how much trouble I was causing you."

He looked down at her, willing himself not to glance at the hand that was still grasping his upper arm. It was a light touch, small, delicate. "Don't worry about it. You saw for yourself, I have free labor."

April shook her head. "I haven't helped you enough to warrant two days' free rent."

"I still have a lot to do around here. I'll exact my pound of flesh."

She wouldn't even smile, just surveyed the supplies and tools crammed around the recliner and then let him go with a jerk, as if she hadn't realized she was still touching him.

"Hey." He waited for her to look at him. "Did you notice if they still have bagels left at the café?"

"They do," she said with a definite lack of enthusiasm. "You'd mentioned breakfast, and I was going to try to tempt you into joining me at the café. The bagels smelled so good, but now—"

"Excellent idea. I'm starving. And I could use more coffee."

"Actually, we should talk."

"We can do that, too." He had no business eating with her. None at all. But he was hungry and he had a full day ahead. "Give me fifteen minutes?"

"Sure. I'll be here."

Both boxes were marked *bathroom*. He picked up the one that contained his toiletries and carried it to his temporary bedroom, wondering how much trouble he could get into in the next two days.

6

"COFFEE, PLEASE," APRIL SAID, her mind shooting in all different directions.

"Is that it, hon?" The waitress didn't even look at her, just waited with her pen at the ready for Luca to order.

April nodded and said, "Yes."

"Make that two coffees," Luca said. "We'll need a minute before we order breakfast."

"No, go ahead. I'm not having anything to eat." April might as well have been talking to the glass case that housed every kind of bagel imaginable. The waitress was already gone and Luca was staring at her as if he was about to dole out a lecture.

"Don't tell me you aren't hungry, because I heard your stomach growling twice."

"No, you didn't."

"Okay, busted. I was trying to be polite. It was more like a dozen times."

She had to smile at that. "We need to be serious," she said, looking into his warm brown eyes and wishing she'd met Luca under different circumstances. Mostly, though, she wished she'd never seen him without a shirt. There was a part of her that wished she'd snapped a pic-

ture of him with her phone. And that wasn't like her at
all. Way too creepy.

"All right." He leaned back in the booth. "What do
you want to talk about?"

"What a selfish person I've been. Yesterday was
clearly not a shining moment for me."

"Because you were yelling and cursing at Wes?"

"Oh, no. I meant every word of that." The waitress
carried a tray of bacon and eggs past their table to the
people behind April and she pressed a hand against her
stomach to keep it quiet. "I shouldn't have begged you
to let me stay. Aside from being rude, it wasn't even
smart. You know, stranger danger and all that."

Luca grinned. "I hope you've gotten past that worry
by now."

"Of course, you've been nothing but a gentleman—"

"Wait," he said, holding up a hand. "Let's decide
on breakfast before the waitress comes back. Then we
can talk."

"I'm only having coffee."

"The hell you are. You promised to help me today. I
don't want you fainting on me."

"Luca—"

"And I should warn you. I don't share."

April bit her lip. "You shouldn't have to, and that's
why I feel so terrible. I wasn't thinking about you at
all last night." Her face heated. After he'd left her last
night, she'd stared at the ceiling reliving the sensation
of his arm around her as he'd helped her up the stairs.
"You know, when I manipulated you," she added.

His slight frown gave her hope. Maybe he didn't
know why she was blushing.

"Okay." The waitress had her pen and notepad out.
"You two ready?"

"April?"

She was better off ordering something to keep Luca off her back. And it did smell awfully good in there. "I'll have the everything bagel with schmear," April said, a little embarrassed at how loudly she'd said that last word. But it was real schmear from New York. On a real New York bagel.

"That it?"

April nodded and the waitress turned to Luca.

"I'll have a plain bagel," he said. "Bacon, two eggs over easy. And hash browns."

"That it?" the woman asked, in the exact same monotone voice.

"And more coffee. For both of us."

"Sure thing. Be right back."

"Um, excuse me." April leaned forward. "May I add two scrambled eggs?"

Scribbling on her pad, the woman said, "You can add anything you want, hon."

"Okay, thanks," April said. The second she turned to go, April said, "I'm sorry," causing her to turn around again. "Could you add some bacon, please? Crispy?"

"Hash browns?"

"No, thanks," April said, leaning back.

"They're really good here," Luca said. "And remember, I don't share."

The woman made a note on her pad and left.

"Does she know I didn't ask for hash browns?"

Luca smiled. "So, this is your first meal in New York."

"And I order bacon and eggs that I could get anywhere." April sighed. "I have to be careful or I'll spend all my money on food. I've been looking up restaurants I want to go to for weeks."

"That's something this city has a lot of. You could eat at a different restaurant every day for two years and not cover them all."

"Well, it's a good thing I like to cook. Assuming I find a place to live with a kitchen." She appreciated him being patient with her, but she wouldn't let the subject drop. "Speaking of which, can you suggest any neighborhoods for me to start searching in? I don't mind sharing, if I have to. And I've got some money, so I'm hoping I won't have to sell my soul to find a decent place in the city."

The way Luca winced didn't portend good news. "Finding a place in Manhattan might be tough. And you'd definitely be sharing with a lot of people."

"What's a lot?"

"Four, five, six?"

"Whoa." That was unexpected. She was hoping to find a place near NYU that she could share with one or maybe two other people.

"Maybe I'm wrong," he said. He wasn't, and they both knew it.

April forced a smile. "Who knows? I might get lucky. In the meantime, however, I've decided to find a small neighborhood motel. Sometimes those places have—"

He was shaking his head.

"What?"

"You're better off focusing on long-term housing."

"Well, I know that, it's just—" She couldn't be more grateful to see the waitress heading toward them with two trays. Or more annoyed when she delivered the food to another table.

April was positive two days wouldn't be nearly enough time for her to get herself situated. She'd been thinking about it ever since she woke up. But that was before…

Damn, she'd been so sure she could convince him that letting her stay in that little room would be a win-win for both of them, just while he remodeled the apartment. And his offer that she help him with his work in exchange for rent had been all the encouragement she'd needed.

"Even in Sunnydale, which is considered one of the least expensive places to live in the city, the rent for a shoebox studio is around a grand," he was saying. "And that's not in Manhattan proper."

"A thousand dollars? A month?"

He nodded. "It's pretty insane. You might have better luck in Brooklyn or Queens. Maybe the Bronx, although I don't know much about the neighborhoods out there. It's not going to be easy."

Every part of her deflated. Even the idea of her genuine New York City bagel couldn't penetrate the feeling of doom that came over her. "I knew it was going to be expensive, but Wes was so sure his friends would be able to help us find something reasonable. I should have done my own research. That absolute swine. I think he lied about everything."

"How long have you known him?"

"Two years. We met at an entrepreneurial workshop at the University of Missouri. A year earlier I'd graduated with a degree in business management, and he has a marketing degree with a minor in information systems. Unless he lied about that, too."

"Sounds like you would have made a great team."

"That's what I thought." She held up both hands. "Surprise!"

"If I could, I'd find him and rough him up for you."

"Thank you. That's a very tempting offer." April smiled, then let a whimper slip. "And how have I repaid you for being so nice? I have a feeling you had your bed put in the small room we cleared in the back. I'm so sorry."

"It fits. So, no problem."

"I had no idea that… I mean you told me last night you were moving in and I didn't even stop to think—"

"April—"

"I was so angry with Wes and worried about what I was going to do." She shook her head and tried to slow her breathing.

"April?"

"You should've kicked me out last night. I would've deserved it but I also would've landed on my feet, because that's who I am. I don't give up easily or—"

"April." He reached across the table and captured her hand.

She stopped fidgeting and swallowed. "What?"

His big, tough hand was surprisingly gentle. Even though she could feel a callus on his palm, it was still a beautiful hand: long, elegant fingers with neatly clipped nails.

April's brain made an easy leap to the image of him from earlier: shirtless, his chest, his shoulders and back bronzed with just the right amount of muscle. He had hair—not too much—sprinkled across his chest and tapering down his flat stomach. Someone could quiz her on the details of his body and she'd pass with flying colors.

They were looking at each other, neither of them saying anything. His eyes seemed darker than before and he wasn't glancing away.

April picked up the glass of water the waitress had

left and took a sip. "Anyway, I really just wanted you to know I'm sorry and that I'll be out by tonight."

Luca finally let go of her hand. "What happened to your offer to help?"

"That was before I realized what a selfish jerk I was being."

"And you remedy that by reneging on our agreement?"

She studied the hard set of his jaw. He looked serious, but he couldn't be. "Do you understand what I'm saying? I'll be out of your hair. For good." The thought made her breath catch. "You'll be able to move your bed and TV upstairs and—" April lost steam. "Luca, you've been incredibly understanding and wonderful to me. I can't… I won't impose on you any longer."

"I had no problem understanding you, but thanks for breaking it down," he said, sounding pissed. "And what I'm telling you is—"

"I don't believe you. Okay? That's the bottom line. You're only saying you need my help to be nice."

"Ah. Okay." He nodded, leaning back, the picture of calm. "Let's assume you're correct. That I'm the great guy you seem to think I am. So how do you think I'd feel about turning you out in a strange city, with little money and no place to go when I have a perfectly good room to offer you?"

"Something's wrong with that logic," April muttered, digging around in her head and coming up short.

"Yeah? Well, it seems logical to me."

He waited for her reply and when she kept quiet, he said, "Look, I'll be back at my job tomorrow, and working on the apartment in the evenings. If you need a few extra days to find a place, it's okay with me."

"Okay," she said finally. "If you're sure." He really

did sound genuine. "I honestly don't mind helping out. I can clean, paint—I've done a lot of painting and light construction before. You can ask me to run errands. Pretty much anything you need. I'm a hard worker. You can count on it. And don't worry, I'll spend every spare minute looking for a place to live."

"I can tell you mean it, and I will ask you to help out."

"Great. I appreciate it so much. I, uh, I'll need to get a phone book, and find a place to get online. Any recommendations?"

"I've got Wi-Fi. I'll give you the password. As long as you don't go streaming Netflix movies, we'll be okay."

She wanted to hug him. Even if he was just being nice because he felt sorry for her. She'd find a way to make it up to him once she was established. Their food arrived, and for a moment, despite everything, she just wallowed in the pleasure of her bagel.

She knew Luca was watching her spread the bounty of cream cheese on her bagel. Probably laughing at her.

"You don't understand," she said. "Where I live, which is a minuscule town outside St. Louis, bagels come from the bread aisle, and even when you do find a restaurant that serves them, they give you this tiny little scoop of cream cheese. It's nothing like this."

She took her first bite. The rich creaminess did a better job of waking her up than the coffee had. Taking her time, she savored each chew and ignored the amusement on Luca's face.

"I take it your expectations have been met."

After she swallowed, she said, "I'm going to gain so much weight here. I'll have to run ten miles a day."

He laughed out loud. "I have a feeling you'll do whatever it takes."

"Well, I'm pretty determined. And kind of sickeningly optimistic. Which probably makes me the mark of the century. God, I still can't believe—"

He found her hand again and covered it with his.

His touch made her tremble inside, which she did her best to stop. Yes, he was gorgeous. Yes, he was being amazingly kind to her, and yes, it was tempting to turn to him for every bit of help she needed, but she wasn't going to. Evidently, she didn't know the first thing about choosing men who could be trusted. She'd be a first-class moron for believing Luca was everything he appeared to be.

"My recommendation? Let it go. I know that sounds like a ridiculous suggestion. That ass has thrown you a curveball that would send most people into therapy. But I already know you can do more than most people. That you're strong, willing to work, smart and not afraid. Center your focus on the next step, and even though it's tempting, don't let what he's done slow you down."

She blinked at him, momentarily forgetting the bagel in her hand, the coffee steaming in her cup, the eggs growing colder by the second. "You must come from a very strong family."

He moved his hand and picked up his fork. "What makes you say that?"

"You sound so levelheaded and normal. Listening to you talk to those guys earlier, I gather you're part of a family business. So, you had a pretty good childhood, then?"

He nodded. "Did you?"

She took another bite of her bagel, because she wasn't sure how much to tell him about herself. She had a tendency to spill everything to anyone who would listen, but that didn't feel very smart to her anymore. "Yes.

My family is great. We're close, and for one reason or another, everyone always ends up back at my parents' house. Not me. I can make it on my own. I have a great business plan, and I'll figure out a way to get out of this mess I'm in. You just watch. I will."

"I believe you," he said with quiet sincerity.

It brought a lump to her throat, and then she reminded herself that she didn't know Luca at all. Instinct told her he was a good guy. But after yesterday, she knew she couldn't even trust herself, much less anyone else. The only thing she was sure of was that he was a smooth talker. And far too hot. Her hand still tingled from where he'd touched her, which was a warning sign as big as Times Square.

"I realize I'm in no position to ask for another favor," she said slowly, and he looked up from his plate, the expression in his eyes making it clear he thought she had some nerve. "But I'm going to, anyway."

He put his fork down and waited.

"When we're working together in the apartment, could you, um, please wear a shirt?"

7

LUCA HAD HOPED to sleep in longer. But he'd forgotten to cover the window of his temporary bedroom, so the morning sun had interrupted a very pleasant dream that had unfortunately starred his sexy upstairs guest.

Maybe he shouldn't have been so generous with his apartment, but it was only for a few days. He believed April meant to charge full speed ahead, and she certainly didn't seem like a quitter, but it wouldn't surprise him if she ended up going back to St. Louis within a week. In the meantime, it would be in his best interest to get any ideas of sex out of his head when she was around. Neither of them needed that complication. It would be inexcusable for him to take advantage of her, anyway.

What he needed to do was think about Jillian. And get rid of his hard-on. Quickly.

Not even a minute in, and his stupid brain turned the channel back to April. As he'd first seen her. The consequences of which had put him in quite a dilemma. Since he was going to gut the bathroom on this floor, he hadn't done anything about the broken shower, so the only full bath available was the one upstairs. But

April was in the bedroom next to the bathroom, and he wasn't going to risk waking her at this ungodly hour.

Which left him with a hard Johnson, a twitching hand and a potential mess.

He could let his erection wither on the vine, and think good, clean thoughts until the problem disappeared…

Yeah, not a chance. He hadn't heard any signs that April was awake yet and she had no reason to come down to this floor so early. And even if she did, well, she was a woman of the world now. A New Yorker. At least for the time being. She'd handle it.

With the image of April in her underwear firmly in mind, it didn't take long for things to come to a conclusion. It occurred to him that one of the reasons he was letting her stay was so that she could help him get the place ready for his date on Thursday night. With beautiful, sexy Jillian. Who hadn't crossed his mind once while he'd…well. That didn't mean anything. And he sure as hell didn't feel guilty about it, either. Not after April's request that he keep his shirt on. The memory of that hadn't gotten old yet, and still made him grin.

Wincing as he stood up in the sweats he'd slept in, he quickly gathered some clothes and toiletries, and made a quick trip through the work area and locked himself inside his bathroom, where he freshened up at the sink. Finally dressed, he headed straight for the coffeemaker he'd bought yesterday and prepared himself a pot.

While the coffee brewed, he made a trip to the corner bodega and picked up a *New York Times* and a bottle of orange juice. Since he had a little time before he had to be at work, he settled into his recliner, turned on ESPN and drank the first cup of his own coffee in his new place.

By the time he got to the sports section, he heard a sound. Several sounds. Louder than they should have been.

It was as if April's footsteps had a direct conduit from the room upstairs to his ears. No wonder her screams had made him think she was so close. The insulation in the ceiling hadn't been replaced yet, and man, it needed to be. The toilet flush was quickly followed by the sound of the shower turning on. He'd put out a mug for her, assuming she'd want coffee, but since he didn't want to think any more about what she was doing upstairs, he went back to reading about his beloved Giants.

Not ten minutes later, he heard her again. Talking. To her mother. He needed to tell April that he could actually hear her. Well, not everything she said. It seemed dependent on where, exactly, she was standing at the moment. Her "Hi, Mom" had been loud and clear, though, and so was her, "Everything's great!"

He understood the lie, but it made him feel bad that she needed to lie at all. It wasn't his problem, however, and he wasn't about to make it any part of his business. Despite the fact that he was giving her a break until she could get on her feet again. The rest of what she said was indistinguishable, but he did hear her laugh—twice, which was good.

He'd really hoped to get to talk to her before he had to leave—particularly so he could mention the noise issue—but when he looked at the scores scrolling across the bottom of the TV screen, his gaze drifted to the time. He needed to get to the Chinatown job site. Pronto.

He put on his steel-toed boots and his jacket then grabbed his hard hat before he went back to the kitchen. No way would he make it all morning on one coffee. Tonight he'd have to dig around and find his to-go cups.

He'd done some more packing at his parents' house yesterday and brought a few more boxes back with him.

As he reached for a mug for his coffee, April's voice drifted through the ceiling. "What do you mean, he's gone to California? We have an appointment tomorrow. I'm just calling to confirm."

Luca winced. Poured himself a half a cup that he tried to drink too quickly, burning his tongue.

"Well, the appointment was with me, not Wes Holland. Right. Thanks, anyway."

Shit, that girl could not catch a break.

Just as he'd taken the last swig of his coffee, the pacing upstairs picked up and an astonished-sounding, "How much?" was followed quickly by an octave-higher, "Per month?"

Guess she hadn't believed him. But New York had a way of becoming real very quickly.

The next thing he heard was footsteps on the staircase. Seeing April in her skinny jeans and tucked-in short-sleeved blouse gave him an inconvenient jolt. Just to change the trajectory of his thoughts he almost made a joke about rental rates in the city, but she looked as though one more blow would have her in tears. "Go ahead," he said. "Have some coffee."

Her smile had him clearing his throat, which reminded him he needed to leave. The job wasn't that far away, but he wanted to be first on site, and it was still possible if he took his Harley.

"There are bagels on the counter. Help yourself."

"Hey, wait a minute," she said, eyeing his clothes and boots, her expression worried. "You're supposed to tell me what I can do for you."

"Nothing right now."

"Two hours of putting down tarps and moving things

around didn't cut it by a quarter. If there's anything else you can think of, please let me know."

"I've got nothing at the moment," he said as he instantly thought of something completely inappropriate. "Keep apartment hunting for today, and we'll talk tonight. Anyway, I'm running late. But good luck."

The last thing he heard was, "Thanks, I'm going to need it."

THE PLACE WAS a sty. The ad had been for a roommate in a one-bedroom apartment. What it hadn't mentioned was that there were already two people living in the 500-square-foot apartment, and the available sleeping spot was a mattress on the floor next to a messy closet. The carpet looked as if it was original to the century-old building and it didn't appear to have been vacuumed. Ever. Still, they were asking $1000 a month. It was enough to make her want to go back to St. Louis and sleep in the barn behind her parents' house. She guessed she wouldn't be looking at places in Manhattan anymore.

Her next stop was in the ritzy Upper East Side neighborhood. Barkingham Palace was an upscale doggy day care and pet salon. It was bright and airy, with aisles devoted to every kind of pet accessory known to man, but the main attraction was the canine clientele. The business housed a spacious area in the back where she spotted a teacup poodle, a Chihuahua, a couple of big Labs and a pair of Rottweilers among half a dozen other pooches.

"April?"

"Mr. Trowbridge?" She recognized him instantly from their conversations over Skype. He was a stocky guy in his midforties, with a smile that had won her over immediately. She had to be careful now with what she said. No way could she tell him about Wes. Not until she had another plan in motion. "It's so nice to finally meet you in person."

He shook his head as he dried his hands. "Call me Alec. You're pretty as a picture. Now, let me give you the tour. It'll have to be fast, though. Lena's out sick today. She's one of our dog washers."

"Oh, I'm sorry. I hope it's nothing serious."

He frowned but shrugged. "She twisted her ankle. Come meet Boone. He's my right-hand man, makes sure we have all our dogs fed according to their owner's instructions and that playtime is well supervised so no one gets too rambunctious. You'll get to know him as he'll work directly with you when our clients are in need of personal services."

God, she hoped so.

They reached the gate leading to the play area. Boone looked to be a little older than she, and very buff, with reddish hair shaved on the sides and styled on top.

"Hey," he said, holding out his hand. "Boone Reardon." His smile was easy but his inspection of her was a little less casual.

She made their handshake brief.

Alec introduced her, and Boone's attitude shifted when he realized she wasn't a client. But it was the way the dogs treated him and vice versa that elevated her opinion of the guy.

Their next stop was the front desk. Angela and Chrissy, also wearing the shop's T-shirts, were both studying at the City College of New York and were cheerful and eager to be of help—exactly the type of people she would want to hire for her business.

"Alec told us about your service," Chrissy said after

she'd rung up a rather extensive wardrobe for a midsize beagle. "I know some people at school who'd be interested. You should come hang out at the student center. I can't guarantee who'll show up, but at least you can leave some brochures or whatever."

"I'd love to." April pulled out a few business cards and wrote down Chrissy's number. She'd have talked longer, but Alec was waiting to show her the next stop on their tour.

The doggy spa was far more glamorous than she could have imagined. Each station had professional lighting and big purple tubs fitted with electric lifts. There were at least eight kinds of shampoo at each station, and she had no idea what half the gadgets lining the tubs were for. Even the drying stations looked like something out of the Jetsons.

There were separate clipping and styling stations, where two men and an older woman were giving some pampered pooches the glam treatment. But the washing area was where Alec hovered, his anxious expression betraying his nerves.

All four washers were wearing heavy-duty aprons that matched the purple tubs, and they all looked like they were enjoying themselves. Two of the stations were empty.

"That's my tub," Alec said, pointing to the one closest to them. "The other one is Lena's. We're booked solid today. I know you're not really a temp agency, but I could really use an assistant if you have a person at the ready. They don't need to be experienced. It's just for the washing and drying, and I'll show them what to do."

"Well, I've only been in town a short time, so we're not quite up and running yet. But maybe I can help?

I'm free for the rest of the day, and I've washed a lot of animals in my time."

"I'm sure you have better things to do—"

"You know what? Working here would add credibility to my recruitment efforts. I'd appreciate the chance, if you'll have me," she said.

"You sure? It can get a little messy."

The truth was she could really use the money. "I promise," she said. "There's nothing I'd rather do today than wash some dogs."

"That's wonderful." Alec was clearly relieved. "I'll explain all there is to do when we get you set up in the break room. Then we'll both go to work and get these dogs looking gorgeous."

Once she was outfitted in her apron and her rubber gloves, she was introduced to her first client—an adorable brindle boxer named Cupcake.

Bathing Cupcake was a piece of...well, cake, and before she knew it she'd done the same with four other dogs: two terriers, a basset hound and a Dalmatian.

Then came Daisy.

"You sure you can handle her?" Alec asked.

"We had a golden retriever when I was a kid," she said. "No problem."

"What would we have done without you today?" Alec said, shaking his head. He helped Daisy into the big tub and scratched the old girl under the chin for a bit. "She's been coming here a long time. She gets the works."

April pet Daisy for a few minutes, letting them get used to each other, then turned on the water. She was convinced that she'd be able to find plenty of students eager to work at the shop, and that thought lifted her spirits quite a bit.

Daisy was as calm as could be as April combed her long coat, grateful that one of the pros would take over when it came time to clip her nails. The dog seemed to enjoy the heck out of getting soaped up from the neck down, and didn't even mind the cotton balls in her ears.

Although she wished Lena a smooth recovery, part of her hoped the woman would be out for a decent stretch, as Alec had already mentioned that April was welcome to step in anytime.

As April was shampooing Daisy's belly, a sharp puppy cry came from behind her. April turned, and that was all it took. One second she was in control, the next, she was soaked from head to toe in dirty dog suds, as Daisy shook all the shampoo off her body.

The laughter didn't help. Peals of it. From the four other groomers and, worst of all, from Alec.

She turned off the tap, but before she had a chance to grab a towel, Alec put one in her hand. "I'm sorry, April," he said. "For what it's worth, it's happened to all of us at one time or another."

"No problem," she said, avoiding opening her mouth too wide in case something unpleasant slipped between her lips. Somehow, she even managed a smile. She was in no position to be picky, so she'd better get used to being slimed.

8

IT WAS FIVE THIRTY when April opened the door to Luca's apartment. It still felt awkward, as if she should knock first, but he'd told her it wasn't necessary. All she wanted to do was race upstairs, get cleaned up and forget about the day she'd just suffered through.

"Whoa," Luca said as she walked into the apartment. He was standing behind his recliner, bottle of water in hand. "You okay?"

She was already several steps up, heading for her room. "Of course I am," she said, not looking back. She took a couple more steps then reversed. "Actually, no. I'm not okay. First, I saw a horrendous apartment that needs to be condemned by the health department.

"And just when I thought my luck had turned because I scored a temp job at a doggy day care, a sweet, old golden retriever slimed me when I was halfway through her bath. Which would have been okay if I hadn't had an interview for a cocktail service job immediately after."

Luca cleared his throat then busied himself turning channels on the muted TV. "Did you get it?"

She held up a dry-cleaner bag. "Got my uniform and

everything. They were dubious, but I swore I didn't normally look, literally, like something the dog dragged in." That was when she noticed the new addition to the kitchen. "Microwave—" she said, pointing.

Luca nodded. "I just picked it up."

It looked so much better than the one upstairs she didn't blame him for ignoring her offer to use it. "I'm sure your refrigerator feels a lot less lonely now."

She came down the remainder of stairs and allowed herself to take in the sight of Luca in his plaid shirt and worn jeans. The tool belt riding low on his hips made her think of what he'd look like without the belt. Or the jeans. "May I take a look? At the microwave?"

"Sure," he said, giving her a quick glance then turning away. "Not that it's any of my business, but do you think there might be a full-time job for you at the doggy day care?"

"I'm not looking for full-time work. I'm going to need time to get my business started."

"Right," he said, turning toward her. "I wasn't thinking."

It hurt her feelings that he'd even asked the question. On the other hand, he didn't really know her, so she couldn't expect him to believe she was serious. "Anyway, I should earn some decent money serving cocktails tonight. I've done it before, back in St. Louis." She shrugged. "It's a private party. I'll be handing out samples of a new brand of vodka cooler. It pays a lot better than most interim work. Nice microwave, by the way."

She turned and headed for the stairs.

"Wait a minute," Luca said. "A private party?"

"That's right." She noticed his frown. But more than that, she noticed how his gaze seemed to be darkening.

She cleared her throat before she continued. "It's at a reputable place. I checked."

"Where is it?"

April put a hand on her hip. His concern was kind of cute—sweet, actually—but for God's sake she wasn't a complete flake. "Despite what you're thinking, I really am capable of taking care of myself."

He looked at the TV screen. "It hadn't crossed my mind that you weren't."

"Although after the whole Wes thing I can understand why you might be skeptical." Annoyed with herself, she sighed. Instead of being cranky she ought to be grateful that he cared. "The company I'm working for tonight handles these promotional events all over the country and I happen to personally know the woman in charge of this region. She hires models for different kinds of events every day. It'll be safe, and the pay is totally worth it."

"Good," he said. "Before you disappear, how about giving me a hand hanging up a curtain?"

She closed her eyes, embarrassed that once again, she'd neglected her deal with Luca. He wasn't worried about her; he wanted her to hold up her end of their bargain as she'd promised. "Of course. Give me two minutes."

She quickly changed into some dry clothes and pulled her wet hair into a messy bun. Then she followed Luca into his makeshift bedroom and stopped dead in her tracks when she saw how much tinier it looked with the bed in it.

"What?" he asked.

"This is terrible. You shouldn't have to sleep in this little bitty space."

"Oh, no. We're not going to have that conversation

again. All we're doing right now is taking this tarp and tacking it up over the window. I need you to stand on this side of the bed and hold one end while I nail my end to the stud."

After slipping her sneakers off, she climbed on top of the bed and took her end of the tarp. It was a pretty crappy curtain, but it would do the trick. Instead of letting guilt swallow her whole again, she focused on holding her arms steady, and watched as Luca hammered in the penny nails.

God, he looked good wielding a hammer. She'd thought a lot about him during the day, about how his muscles rippled when he moved, and how she had no business thinking about him at all.

Then he got up on the bed next to her. Close enough that she could actually see the sweat beading on his five-o'clock shadow. A lock of errant hair kept falling over his brow, and her fingers itched to brush it back.

After he'd finished with the middle section, he moved even closer to her. She closed her eyes, inhaling his clean, masculine scent, different from this morning, but just as enticing.

"Uh, April?"

"Yes?" she said, her voice just a little breathless.

"It's drooping."

She quickly lifted her end of the tarp just as he reached over to do the job himself. He'd bent just enough to bring his face right next to hers, and when she felt his breath, she turned and there were his eyes, staring. His lips so close they were almost kissing.

It was impossible not to lean in that tiny inch more. But when her lips touched his, she gasped, he jerked and she almost fell off the bed.

She let go of the tarp, jumping down, somehow not

killing herself in the process. "I'll let you finish up," she said, her face flaming.

"Yes. Right. I'll, uh—"

She made it out of the room in two seconds flat, only realizing she'd left her sneakers next to his bed when she was halfway up the stairs.

LUCA PULLED OUT his keys, shaking his head as he unlocked the garage he'd rented for the past four years. More than just a place to stash his Harley, it was his workshop, the one he never talked about.

The garage was his Sanctum Sanctorum, where he came to clear his mind, to get lost in creating the furniture that hit the sweet spot deep inside him. It was where he came when his parents were driving him crazy, which happened a lot during the long winter months. Hell, pretty much all the time.

After flipping on the lights, he rested his hand on his bike, the smooth black paint as shiny as the day he'd bought it.

The irony of his visit tonight wasn't lost on him. After all the trouble he'd gone through to get his own place so he could finally do whatever the hell he wanted, whenever he wanted, and what had happened?

April.

April had happened to him. Was still happening to him. Would continue to happen for as long as he let her stay, or until she found herself a place to live. He really hoped she'd find an apartment soon because asking her to leave was going to be a bitch.

In the meantime, she had to go and smell like coconut and flowers. It was difficult enough, her wearing skinny jeans. The way they cupped her ass, hugged her hips. Damn. But now that she would be wearing those skimpy outfits to her "events"? As if he needed to know exactly what her legs looked like. In heels.

"Shit."

It was more than he could handle. He was bound to do something that would freak them both out. It had almost happened last night…which was precisely why he'd decided to come straight to the garage after work.

All day he'd been flashing back to last night, in his bedroom, nose to nose with April, breathing in her breath, watching her pupils dilate as they moved into the kiss that wasn't.

What the hell was wrong with him? It hadn't only been a bad idea, it had also become an idea that wouldn't stop looping through his brain. Worse than an earworm, worse than remembering an embarrassing mistake that clung like a burr. Every time he thought about those lips so close, his brain went directly to his list of biggest regrets.

He walked back to his work space. His latest project was a patio table that also served as a cooler. Eight square feet of cedar, fitted with a long plastic planter frame he'd retrofit so it could hold ice. He still had to finish the legs, which would be the perfect job to distract him.

With any luck at all, he'd get home after April was sound asleep upstairs.

As he prepped the first leg for the router, his cell phone rang. Turning off the equipment, he checked the number. It was one of his construction supervisors. "Hey, Dave. Everything okay?"

"Yeah, sure. No problems. I know it's late, but I wanted to catch you before I leave town. You got a minute?"

"Of course."

"You know the Mostel job? Mrs. Mostel?"

"The remodel in SoHo."

"Yeah. She saw that entertainment unit you made for the Rothenbergs, and she flipped. She said, and I quote, 'The work is masterful. The man's a genius.'"

"What can I say? The woman's got taste."

Dave laughed. "Hey, I think she has a keen eye, and I'm not just saying that. Anyway, she was hoping to meet with you, get you to do some custom pieces for her new place. She mentioned a dresser, a table and a hutch to go with one of her antique cabinets. For what it's worth, the lady's loaded."

Shit. Money might not be a problem for her, but time was a problem for him. He put in a lot of hours for the business, and as much as he loved working with his hands, if he took on more private clients, he'd have little time to enjoy his new place. And all the sex he was hoping to have in the near future.

The thought alone had him picturing April. Of course. Because he clearly wasn't at his breaking point yet.

He held back a sigh and closed his eyes. Wouldn't hurt to talk to the woman. "Why don't you give me her number, and I'll give her a call later."

"Great. I actually gave her one of your cards, but I'll tell her you'll call as soon as you can."

"Thanks, Dave."

"Hey, if I could afford you, I'd hire you, too."

Luca laughed as he disconnected then shook his head. Flattery wasn't going to take care of his problems. It seemed that his best laid plans were absolutely no use in getting him laid at all.

When he finally did go home, April was there in her tiny shorts and too-small T-shirt, which might as well have been soaking wet for how it clung to her body.

He simply couldn't win.

9

LATE THE NEXT AFTERNOON, after he'd showered and changed, Luca headed out the door, glad he had beat April home. He wasn't taking any chances that she'd worked at the dog groomer's today. It was hard enough living in such close quarters without her clothes leaving next to nothing to the imagination.

The elevator door opened and he knew who it was right away. Jesus. She was driving him crazy, coming home looking like that. "Hey," he said. "I see you're still working at the dog spa."

April paused and shifted her tote bag on her shoulder, which didn't help matters. "Yep. For now."

She started walking toward him and he made sure to meet her eyes, but she looked away.

"I also looked at two apartments today, and they both had roaches everywhere and I'm pretty sure one was a drug den. But I've got more lined up, and also I've got three more event bookings, so I promise, I haven't been slacking. And Alec could call me again for tomorrow. It depends."

"Alec? The dog spa owner?"

"Yes. But I don't want to hold you up…" She raked a

gaze over his leather jacket to the helmet tucked under his arm. "You have a motorcycle?"

"A Harley. Going for a ride tonight, then I have to work on a project. What about you?"

"I've got an event later."

Excellent. He'd come back and work on the living room after she left. He wasn't making enough progress before his big date with Jillian. "Well, good luck," he said and started to pass April, but stopped. "Look, in the spirit of camaraderie, I should tell you something."

"Oh, God. Did you need me to help you and I wasn't here? I'm so sorry. I'm here now until nine. I'll do whatever you want."

Luca closed his eyes, but that just made things worse. Images popped into his head. Bad, bad images. "Okay, here's the thing. Every time you come back from the groomer's, it looks like you've been in a wet T-shirt contest," he said, waiting for it to register. "And it's gotten to the point where I want to ask you if you won."

April's eyes got wide. Then she looked down. Straight down. At her very prominent nipples. Her breasts weren't that big, but those nipples… Suffice it to say they were highly distracting.

"Oh, God." She spun around and dashed past him into the apartment, but not before he caught the brilliant blush that painted her cheeks.

He wasn't in great shape himself. When he looked south, his erection was pretty damn obvious. Terrific. His only hope was that she'd been too busy blushing to notice.

The door swung back open before he'd gone two steps.

"Wait a minute," she said. "Does that mean you really think I could have won?"

Luca groaned and hurried to the elevator. What the hell was he going to do with that woman?

Not what he wanted to do, that was for sure.

THE BREAK ROOM off the kitchen didn't have many available tables, but April was so grateful to get off her feet she wouldn't have cared if she'd had to sit on the floor.

She'd been on the move since the minute she'd arrived at the Top-of-the-Rock, a gorgeous sky-high space at Rockefeller Center, where she was serving cocktails for a silent charity auction. There were over a hundred people there, all of them rich as hell and, so far, well behaved.

"Can you believe this place?" Grace, another cocktail server, sat down next to her. "All I want to do is look at the view."

April took advantage of the cheese and fruit platter left out for the staff and grabbed a couple of cubes of Gouda. "It's stunning. Have you worked at this venue before?"

Her new friend was a gorgeous blonde. She was wearing the same skin-tight black dress as April, and the required six-inch heels that made her tower over nearly everyone. "Last year, for another silent auction. The pay was great, but I barely had a chance to sit down."

April didn't dare remove her shoes for fear of not being able to put them on again. She'd be sore as could be tomorrow, which was scary because she'd booked a far less elegant event where she'd be run ragged. "If I never had to wear heels again, that would be fine with me."

"I know," Grace said. "At least it's halfway over. I think I might've seen you at the agency before."

"I'm just doing this so I can save enough money to get an apartment, but this city is insane."

"Huh." Grace smiled at her and plucked a slice of apple off the plate. "Where are you looking?"

"I've pretty much given up finding anything in Manhattan proper. Now I'm checking out Brooklyn, Queens, and I've got an appointment across the bridge in New Jersey the day after tomorrow. At least I know now not to believe everything I read. My God, some of them were terrifying."

"I know what you mean," she said. "I dreaded every viewing when I moved here from Wyoming."

"Did you live on a ranch?"

"Nope. In Jackson Hole."

"I lived in a rural area outside St. Louis with just enough animals to be a pain in the butt."

"So do you like it here in the city?"

April nodded. "I do. It's an adjustment, though. I'm overstaying my welcome where I'm at now, so I've got to make a move. Fast."

"Not to get your hopes up too high, but I might have a space available at my place in a week."

April perked up, crossing her metaphorical fingers. "Really?"

"I'll warn you, it's a long commute. The place is nice, but it's a one-bedroom, so that means you'd be sleeping on a pullout couch. The kitchen's not bad, though, and the area is safe."

"When you say long commute…"

Grace's perfect nose scrunched up. "I work at the Seagram's building, and the train takes almost two hours each way. On the plus side, it's pretty much my only time to chill. I read or sleep."

"You feel comfortable enough to sleep?"

"Not all the time, no. But I made sure to introduce myself to the regulars who go out to Perth Amboy. We watch out for each other."

A quick glance at her watch told April it was time to go back to work. "I'd like to get your number before I leave tonight. Maybe we can talk?"

"Sure, but again, it's not for sure. My current roommate is almost certain she's got a job in California, but it's not a done deal."

Tell you what, maybe we could get a drink next week, when I know more. I get off work at 6:00 p.m. We can find a place that's convenient for both of us."

Wincing as she stood up, April ran a hand through her hair and refreshed her lipstick before she had to grab her tray loaded with glasses of the best champagne she'd ever tasted. They were each allowed a tiny sample and then instructed never to have another sip. The auction was for works of art that ran into the millions, all to benefit a program that funded a major Alzheimer's research facility.

Thankfully, she was used to dealing with the upper crust, who weren't afraid to ask her to do favors for them. One woman wanted her to call her nanny to make sure her children were safely tucked in for the night. As instructed, April did her best to accommodate every request, always remembering that the pay was commensurate with the level of service provided.

By the time the auction was in full swing, she'd been switched from serving champagne to offering tiny extravagant desserts, which made her wish she'd eaten more on her break. Every second she had for a spare thought, her mind immediately went to Luca first, and she had to force herself to reflect on her conversation with Grace instead.

April really liked Grace, and even though Perth Amboy might be a two-hour commute, she definitely wanted to check out the apartment, if the space became available. The need to move was becoming critical.

Not that Luca would ever say as much, but it was clear to her that he wanted his space back. She couldn't blame him. He'd gone above and beyond to let her stay so long, and she'd be forever grateful. But the tension between them was getting thicker by the day, exacerbated by her ever-growing attraction to him. It was so bad that his avoiding her was both a blessing and a curse.

God, she was going to miss him. His smile. The way he joked with her. How he made her feel.

Realizing she'd stopped circulating, she got her head back in the game. She needed to be the perfect employee tonight, so she'd be hired for more events of this caliber. Even if it meant wearing six-inch heels every night of the week.

THE NEXT MORNING April promised herself that no matter what happened, she wouldn't allow anything to dampen her enthusiasm. But after wasting several hours looking at three studio apartments in Queens, all of them competing for the most awful efficiency east of the Mississippi, she conceded that she may have been too ambitious.

At 3:30 p.m., she hurried toward Luca's apartment, hoping to beat him home. Other than two rounds of dog-walking duty for Alec, she hadn't taken any other paying jobs for the day. She'd been in New York less than a week and she needed to concentrate on getting out of Luca's place.

Her five-day extension was up. He hadn't offered to

let her stay longer. In fact, he hadn't mentioned anything at all. And neither had she, but aside from it being unfair to Luca to continue mooching off him, the uncertainty of her future was beginning to weigh on her.

"Hey, April."

Recognizing the voice, she turned and waved at Carmen who was standing in the doorway of the bodega where she worked.

"Any luck today?"

April shook her head, trying to decide if it would be too rude to keep walking. Normally she'd stop and chat. She'd met three people in the neighborhood so far: Carmen and two shop owners. All very nice women who'd promised to let her know if they heard of any available apartments that rented for less than the national debt.

A customer entering the store settled the dilemma. Carmen waved and followed the man inside. April hurried to the apartment. She let herself in the front door and looked around at the relatively clutter-free floor. She wondered how long he'd been home. Most of the tarps and drop cloths were folded and stacked in the corner. A card table and two folding chairs had been set up next to the wall near the window, and as she got closer, she saw it was covered with blueprints. They were the plans for this level, and while she didn't want to snoop, she figured the page underneath was the upper floor.

Not that she was an expert, but she understood the basics of blueprints, and it was fascinating to get an idea of what the finished kitchen would look like. But even more interesting to her was the information in the title block at the top of the page. These were Luca's drawings. She'd known he did construction, but clearly that wasn't all. Wow.

She was about to call out to him when she saw a note taped to the side of the fridge. It read:

April, I'll be out for the evening. If you could finish cleaning up the kitchen, and wash the floor, that would be great. See you later. And thanks!

Her spirits plunged even further, although she was glad he'd given her something to do until it was time to go to her event that night. But she'd miss seeing him. A lot.

10

"HEY." LUCA TURNED and smiled as she shut the door behind her.

April almost asked him what he was doing here. After he'd pulled disappearing acts three nights in a row, she hadn't expected to see him. "Hi."

"You did a great job on the floor yesterday," he said, although how he could tell was a mystery. Packing materials were scattered all over. "Don't worry, I'm going to clean all this up."

April shrugged. "It's your apartment."

He'd opened up a box of glass tiles that she knew would end up as a backsplash. "You working tonight?"

"Nope. Let me run upstairs real quick and then I'll be ready to help."

"I'll take you up on that."

After she changed and put her hair in a ponytail she joined him, and while they worked installing a water filter kit and preparing the wall for the backsplash, she found out more about Paladino & Sons, and Luca's brothers, Tony and Dom.

It sounded as if their company was big all over Lower Manhattan, and she wished she had more experience doing construction work. It paid really well, and she never did mind the physical labor.

A couple hours went by quickly. There was a lot of bumping into each other and accidental touching. Each touch was a jolt, every brush an exercise in restraint. Considering that, she was pleased that she'd managed to make it this far without tearing his clothes off. Okay, maybe she was being overly dramatic. But even with the chilly autumn wind blowing through Little Italy, they hadn't needed to turn on the furnace, which said something.

"What's next?" she asked after washing her hands.

"Basically I'd like to make the place as presentable as possible," he said, his brows lowering as he looked around. "So, you know, dusting, scrubbing the sinks, whatever it takes."

"Got it," she said, though his sudden anxiousness made no sense to her. Since he'd had plenty of chances to explain what the big rush was about and had chosen not to, she didn't feel comfortable asking.

He used the back of his shirtsleeve to blot the sweat above his brow. "Are you going to be around tomorrow morning?"

"I am."

"And you have that event you're working in the evening, right?"

She gave him a polite nod, accompanied by an equally polite smile, and refrained from pointing out that he'd asked the same question twice now. Her curiosity was approaching the point of no return. If he asked again, he'd open a floodgate of nosy questions about why he was so interested in getting his work space so clean. No matter what they did, the place would still look like a construction zone.

Was someone coming over? His parents, maybe? His brothers? They were all in the same business, so they wouldn't expect the apartment to be spotless. She'd dismissed the idea of a date. Not at this stage of the re-model. And honestly, it was just too upsetting to pic-ture him with a woman.

Wait… Could he just be creating work for her? The floor? Dusting?

She wouldn't ask. If this was what he wanted her to do, then fine. It made her life much easier, because every hour of work she put in meant she panicked a little less about paying him back.

"I'm ready for a beer," he said. "How about you?"

"Thanks, but I think I'll stick with water." She watched him walk to the fridge, her mind going back and forth, grateful he'd kept his shirt on and wishing he hadn't. "By the way, I've been keeping track of the extra days I've stayed because you're definitely get-ting the short end of the stick. I haven't done enough to offset rent," she said. "After seeing what kinds of shit holes are on the market and knowing what people are actually paying for them…"

"That's New York for you." He twisted off the cap and took a pull of beer.

"I wonder if that's what spooked Wes."

Luca lowered the bottle and looked at her. "Have you heard from him?"

"Not a word." She hadn't meant to speculate out loud. And now Luca was looking at her funny. "I don't expect to, either. And I'm not making excuses for him. Or try-ing to rationalize his behavior in any way. It's just—" She shrugged. "I'd just like to know why."

Luca nodded and took another swig.

"If not for you, I honestly don't know what I would've

done. That being said, I feel obligated to remind you that my five extra days are up and we haven't talked about when you'd like me to vacate."

At his slow smile her heart lurched.

"Yeah, I know you wish I was gone already," she muttered and uncapped her water, suddenly nervous that he might tell her tomorrow would be good.

"I didn't say that."

"Of course you didn't, because that's not who you are."

He laughed. "We have different memories of that first night."

"Oh, no, I remember. But who could blame you? Anyway—" April relaxed a little and paused to take a drink.

"Not now, okay? I need to get this place in—" He went utterly still and just stared at her. "Oh, for Christ's sake," he muttered. "Are you kidding me?"

"What are you talking about?" Following his gaze, she looked down at her shirt. A tiny trickle of water had dribbled down right between her breasts. It wasn't a big deal. Not even close to a day of shampooing dogs. "Are you serious?"

"We just talked about this, April," he said through gritted teeth.

"It wasn't on purpose and this doesn't even show anything." She brushed her fingers over the damp spot and saw that her nipples were sticking out. "Oh."

"Yeah. Exactly."

Shaking his head, he took a huge gulp of his beer. The dual action caused the same thing to happen to him. He glared at the beer soaking into the front of his shirt.

April bit back a laugh.

"Don't say it."

"I don't know what you mean. Besides, things will settle down for me in a minute," she said, plucking at her shirt. "So, in the meantime, how about you just don't look?"

"Right. Good plan."

She'd never seen him roll his eyes before. She lowered her gaze, stiffened and pretended she'd missed the impossible-to-miss bulge behind his fly. Turning away, she asked, "Is there a hardware store nearby?"

"Around the corner. Why?"

"I'd like to take another pass at the floor but I need to get a few things."

He got out his wallet.

"That's okay. I've got this." Famous last words. She ran upstairs, grabbed her jacket and wallet and flew back down.

Luca hadn't moved, and she swore on everything she held sacred she wouldn't look *there*.

"You want directions?" he asked as she put her hand on the doorknob.

She nodded and held her breath while memorizing what he told her.

She made it to the store ten minutes before closing. Hands down, it was the smallest hardware store she'd ever seen, with narrow aisles and merchandise crammed tightly together. With rents being what they were, she wasn't surprised. It didn't take her long to find the cleaner her mother had used forever, along with a good mop, then she took her place at the register.

"April?" The male voice coming from behind was unfamiliar. And April wasn't an unusual name. "April Branagan?"

At that, she turned around and immediately recognized the tall, dark-haired man. "Hello, Officer…"

"Ferrante." He grinned. "I didn't have to arrest you, so call me Vinny."

"Gee, thanks," she said, "for reminding me of the worst day of my life."

"Hey, we were all sweating it. A big unattended bag like that…"

"I know. You can't imagine how sorry and embarrassed I am over the incident. Honestly, I should probably bake cookies or something and take it to your precinct."

A paunchy older man sauntered over from the aisles and squeezed behind the counter. "Is this it for you?" he asked.

"I hope so." She hadn't quite calmed down yet and it wouldn't surprise her if she had forgotten something. "What time do you open tomorrow?"

He nodded at the sign by the door. "Nine o'clock, just like I have for the last thirty years."

"And just like you will for the next thirty," Vinny said, standing awfully close to her.

"Nah, the old ticker or next rent hike will get me first." He scanned the price code on the mop she held up for him.

"Come on, Gus, when was the last time you had an increase?" Vinny asked. "Most of the businesses on the block haven't gone up in years."

"Wow, that's hard to believe." April opened her wallet. "Rent is the new four-letter word for me."

"That's right. You're from St. Louis."

Gus gave her a total and she passed him some bills. Holy cow! Even the most basic household stuff was expensive.

"You still staying at the Mercury Building?" Vinny

asked, and she nodded. "Who did you say you were visiting?"

"Knock it off, Vinny. Quit hustling my customers." Gus gave her a kind wink along with her change.

The cop put her on edge when he brushed against her hip, but she hated that her nervous reaction was obvious.

"What you got there, Officer?" Gus leaned over the counter to see what he was holding. "I'd get a better snow shovel than that. I got a shipment coming in three weeks."

"What about the generator?" Vinny threw her a glance as she hurriedly gathered her purchases. "Wait. I'll only be a minute."

She pretended she hadn't heard him and slipped out of the store. Even if she wasn't interested in making a fast getaway, the brisk air would've propelled her along the sidewalk past a bakery and the bodega where Carmen worked. The talk about snow shovels made her want to curl into a ball for the entire winter. She was used to snow—that wasn't the problem. Not knowing where she'd be living once the really bad weather hit was the upsetting part. It seemed each new apartment she looked at was taking her farther and farther from the city.

She waited forever for the elevator, and by the time it came she'd decided to ask Luca straight out why the manic cleaning was so important. It was a legitimate question because she needed to know how soon she had to wash the floors. She really hoped it could wait until tomorrow.

After knocking the hell out of the elevator car and corridor walls with the unwieldy mop handle, she got to Luca's door and realized she didn't have the key with her.

Damn. Damn. Damn.

She knocked.

When he didn't answer, she knocked again.

"Hey, April. Wait."

She jerked so hard she lost her grip on the mop. It was Vinny. How the hell...

He'd just gotten off the elevator and was walking toward her.

Luca opened the door. And he wasn't wearing a shirt.

She wanted to smack him, but with Vinny as a witness, she'd end up being charged with assault.

"Forget your key?" he asked with a half grin.

"Forget your shirt?"

"Paladino?" Another step and Vinny would've run into her. What was he thinking? "Luca, right?"

He nodded, looking confused. "You're...Auggie's brother."

"Yep, that's me, the good-looking one," Vinny said, laughing. His gaze bounced between them, then he sized up Luca's bare chest. "Are you two—"

"No." Luca's quick and emphatic denial was a bit insulting.

April just smiled and shook her head.

"Cool," Vinny said, his eyes narrowing at Luca's naked torso before turning to grin at her. "For a short little thing you can move. I didn't think I'd catch you."

"Did I drop something?" April asked, all innocent.

Luca stood in the doorway, unsmiling and unmoving.

Apparently only Vinny didn't find the moment growing more awkward by the second. "You want to go out sometime?" he finally asked. "I can show you the sights, we can have a little dinner..." He flashed her a smile that would've been killer on any other guy. "Give me your number. We can talk later."

April didn't know what to do. She didn't want to go

out with Vinny but it would've been easier to turn him down without Luca standing there as if he was guarding Fort Knox.

"Ah, that's so nice of you to offer but I'll be leaving New York soon."

"Well, that's too bad." Vinny shrugged. "Take it easy," he said and left. She turned back to the door and almost plowed into Luca. "Excuse me," she said and pushed past him.

He took the mop from her. "Did you mean it?"

"Mean what?" She carried her supplies into the kitchen.

"Are you really leaving or did you just say that to Vinny?"

His tone was completely neutral. She couldn't tell if he was relieved or upset or ready to jump up and down with joy. She wanted to turn around and see his face when she answered. But if he looked disappointed when she admitted it was a small fib, it would crush her.

"Kind of both," she said, slowly turning to face him. Something in his eyes made her heart stop. It was as if he'd just gotten terrible news. But one blink later and he seemed completely unaffected.

Afraid she'd give her own feelings away, she made the idiotic mistake of lowering her gaze to his chest. His pectorals bunched and released, the subtle movement making her pulse race.

No matter how she looked at it she had to get out of this apartment before she did something she'd regret forever.

11

As soon as April had left to work an event the next evening, Luca got a move on. He showered and shaved then made sure his blueprints were set out to show Jillian.

The whole ride over to the Korean restaurant in the Village, he kept reminding himself that it was none of his business who April wanted to go out with. He and April didn't owe each other anything. No explanations. No excuses. Although if she changed her mind and decided to go out with Ferrante, he was going to have a serious talk with her. That slick bastard had one hell of a nasty reputation with women. Vinny could make Wes look good.

Luca smiled. That was exactly how he'd put it to April. The guy wouldn't stand a chance after that.

Then again, she'd said she was leaving New York soon, and that was far more troubling than Vinny Ferrante. It should have been good news. Finally, he'd be able to live the dream.

Dammit. He'd be sorry to see her go, though. In spite of the fact that she was slowly killing him with frustration.

Jillian was just about to slide into a booth on the

other side of the restaurant when he arrived at K'OOK.
Tall, curvy, with a bright smile and a short cropped Afro
that made her green eyes seem luminous, she looked
as great as she had the last time he'd seen her. Before running into her at the Zaha Hadid retrospective,
he hadn't seen her since they'd been students. They'd
never hooked up back in school, but two weeks ago the
chemistry between them had been palpable, and while
they hadn't done anything but get a drink, he'd made
the date before they parted.

"I'm not late, am I?" he said, sliding in next to her.

"Not at all. I just got here myself." She hadn't left
him much room—their thighs didn't quite touch but
almost. Always a positive sign.

"How was your trip?"

"Oh, my God…" Her face lit up. "Have you been to
Barcelona?"

"Only Madrid."

"You've got to make it to Barcelona sometime. The
architecture is crazy," she said, and just like that they
fell into easy conversation. He'd always enjoyed Jillian's sense of humor, and they both laughed a lot as
they reminisced about their college days.

An hour later everything about the evening pointed
to a happy ending. That was, if he didn't blow it all to
hell and back. He'd almost brought up April several
times, stopping himself before he blundered.

"Would you like dessert? Another drink?"

Jillian put her hand on his arm. "No, thanks. It was
all delicious, but I'm anxious to see your plans."

It was the fourth time she'd touched him in the same
place, and what that signaled made him rush to pay the
bill. "You haven't told me much about your internship,"

he said as they walked out of the restaurant to hail a taxi. "Are you liking it?"

She shrugged her shoulders, which emphasized her breasts. "I expected a more hands-on approach, but that could be the company. Maybe other firms treat their interns differently. Guess you'll find out soon enough."

"Yeah," he said, glad a cab pulled over. Two weeks ago he'd told her about the Willingham offer. He sure didn't want to discuss it now. They got in and inched their way through the evening traffic. They sat close to each other. Talked. Smiled. Touched. It was all looking good, although he guessed the real sparks would fly once they got comfortable at his place.

Once they entered his apartment, Jillian stood near the door as she looked around. "Wow, it's huge. How in the world did you score this place?"

Used to sidestepping the question, Luca just smiled. "I've already taken down two walls." He stashed her jacket and purse and took her on a quick tour. "I've barely started on the bathroom and kitchen on this level."

"What's back there?"

"Currently it's my bedroom but eventually it'll be an office. Let me show you upstairs first."

"Remind me about what you're doing up here?" Jillian asked when they got to the second floor.

"Most of it will be my master bedroom suite and a screened-in porch. And possibly a small guest room on the other side. I haven't decided yet." He'd made sure April's door was shut before he'd left the apartment. But he should've anticipated the question.

Jillian stopped at the closed door. "Is this a bedroom?"

"Yes. Unfortunately, it's occupied at the moment.

Hey, you know Jefferson Holt? From Columbia? He studied architecture for a while."

"He sounds familiar."

"Well, anyway, he asked me to rent a room to a buddy of his since I hadn't started on the remodel yet. Bad move. Last time I do him a favor."

Jillian grinned and, luckily, dropped the subject as he finished showing her around. He tensed, realizing he hadn't inspected the bathroom before he'd left, and awkwardly darted in ahead of Jillian. No bra or thong hanging off the towel bar, thank God.

April had only left her underwear on display one time. Thinking about her reaction that morning made him smile. He quickly sobered when Jillian gave him a funny look.

When they returned to the kitchen, he poured some wine. Together, they stood over the blueprints, going over the minutia that interested the architect in them both. She asked great questions and gave him a couple of good ideas.

Luca wished he could relax and get more into it. From the moment he'd opened his front door, thoughts of April kept creeping into his head. She wouldn't even be home until after 2:00 a.m., but that wasn't the problem. April had only been there a week, but somehow she'd become a part of his life. It wasn't just the towel rod that had him thinking of her. The gleaming floor, the stacks of tarp, the damn refrigerator. All of it was associated with a moment, a look, a conversation, that was etched in his memory. But he couldn't afford to think about her now. He'd been planning this date for too long.

After he'd finished showing Jillian the drawings for the patio, she met his gaze with a mischievous wink.

"It sounds fantastic." Stepping closer, she moved her elegant fingers to the top button of his shirt, slipping it open with ease. "I'll be interested to see how it turns out."

The next button was conquered as Luca put his hands on her waist. She'd worn a formfitting dress that hugged her in all the right places. Given the circumstances, he should be the one doing the undressing, but all he could think was that whatever spark had been there when they'd bumped into each other at the gallery had dimmed. A lot.

So, what the hell? Obviously it was just him. It had never occurred to him that he wouldn't be 100 percent up for this night. He'd really looked forward to it.

But now? He let his hands drop to his sides. "Listen, Jillian…"

She tilted her head to the right, the same thing April did when she wasn't sure what he was going to say.

"I hate to do this to you, especially when you look so beautiful and you've been so great, but do you think we could put this on hold and do it again in a week or so?"

She let out a soft exhale. "No, I don't mind. Are you sure you want to reschedule?"

"Yeah, of course."

"Huh," she said, taking a couple of steps back so she could pick up her wineglass. "Let me guess. Jefferson's buddy's name is April."

Luca blanched. He darted a look around the kitchen, trying to figure out how he'd tipped his hand.

"It's just… You've called me April," Jillian said, her smile gone wry. "Twice."

He briefly closed his eyes. "Jillian, I'm so sorry—"

"It's fine. Honestly. I know how uncomfortable it can be to have houseguests." She abandoned her wine to fetch her coat and purse. "It was a lovely dinner, and I very much approve of your renovation plans."

He walked her to the door, embarrassed at his behavior and how much he'd let April get inside his head. Jillian deserved better.

Jillian just chuckled. "Good night, Luca," she said and crossed the threshold into the hall.

Luca stepped out to say good-night, but the words stuck in his throat. Why the hell was April back so early? Her job was supposed to go until at least 1:00 a.m.

As Jillian passed her, she gave April a quick once-over before continuing to the elevator.

APRIL WATCHED THE woman hit the elevator button, certain she was witnessing the end of a successful date. Her hunch was confirmed when she turned back to Luca, his shirt halfway unbuttoned. "Sorry I interrupted," she said, rushing past him and quickening her steps to the stairs.

She closed her bedroom door with a little too much force, but it didn't matter. So much made sense now. The way he'd wanted to clean up the place, asking her over and over if she would be working. How he'd avoided being alone with her.

There was absolutely no reason for her gut to be churning, for the fierce waves of jealousy that were crashing inside her. Luca wasn't her boyfriend. So there'd been some tension between them. It had clearly meant nothing.

The knock on the door didn't surprise her, but she didn't answer it. Instead, she got out her big suitcase and started folding up her jeans.

Luca opened the door, but stayed in the hallway. "April? Listen, I—"

"I found a place to stay," she said, careful not to look at him. "I'm moving."

"Where?" He sounded shocked, though probably not half as stunned as she felt. But she couldn't bear to stay now.

"What difference does it make? You should be thrilled. I'll be out of your hair for good." She yanked blouses off their hangers and tossed them in the suitcase. She'd been using it as a drawer, so most of her stuff was already neatly folded inside.

"How did you find an apartment in the last four hours?"

"Again, irrelevant." She scooted around the bed when she noticed he was moving closer. "For what it's worth, I really am sorry if I screwed up your date. She must be someone special," April said, eyeing his chinos and gaping gray shirt.

"Nothing happened."

April paused, her green T-shirt halfway folded. It shouldn't feel this good, knowing Luca wouldn't lie. Which didn't negate the fact that she'd let things get way too complicated. Even if she'd had to stay at a dive, she should have left after two days.

Oh, God. She still resented making the floor shine just so he could impress that woman. Whether they'd had sex or not. And after he'd been so nice to her.

She gathered all her makeup and threw it in a bag, pissed at herself, at him, at Wes, at life. Then she shouldered past him to get her toiletries from the bathroom. On her way out she grabbed a roll of toilet paper. "Here," she said, startled to see him in the hall waiting for her. "For the one I borrowed." She tossed the roll at him.

He didn't try to catch it. The toilet paper just bounced off his jaw. "What the hell?"

"I didn't mean for that to happen. You were supposed to catch it."

"Nothing's your fault, is it?" He shoved a hand through his hair, his eyes dark and unyielding. "You never mean for anything to happen."

"Oh, that's low, even for you." April spun around with every intention of locking herself in the bathroom.

She gasped when he caught hold of her arm and spun her back around. "What are you doing?"

Luca gave her a slight tug, but it was enough to bring her too close. "You're driving me crazy," he said, staring at her as if she were made of secrets. "Do you have any idea—" he said, his words so low she might have missed them if she hadn't been just inches away. He opened his mouth once more, only to pull her into a kiss.

Oh, God.

His lips, warm, urgent, on hers. His arms suddenly wrapped around her, holding her tight. His tongue seeking entry, teasing her to open her mouth.

All coherent thought vanished. April abandoned herself to her feelings. This was bliss. It was what she'd wanted since the second night. This kiss, this heat, this electricity between them. It wasn't smart, but she didn't give a damn. Not when it felt so perfect.

Touching his hard chest ramped things up even more. And when he changed the position of the kiss, she let out an embarrassing squeak, but he didn't stop.

His hands moved down her back to her waist then up again while he worked magic with his mouth. She tasted a hint of wine and something that belonged to Luca. *Him.* She wanted to take everything in. His scent, his strong body against hers, his erection growing and pulsing between them.

Her arms went around his neck, and she pressed her

breasts to his chest, making him inhale sharply before he took her mouth again. She groaned in surrender, his tongue thrusting and tasting, telling her all he wanted them to do. Showing her when his hands moved underneath her T-shirt, cool on the bare skin of her back.

He wasn't "the one"—he couldn't be, not after everything that had happened. She knew better than to believe that fairy tale. But the way he kissed sure made her want to believe.

Luca pulled back, his breathing ragged, desperate, as he peered into her eyes. His lips were parted, moist, his eyes dark with desire.

She knew she should stop this. Right this second, before they both did something they couldn't take back.

But then he kissed her again, harder this time, hard enough to make her whimper. The vibration from his guttural moan was so intimate and erotic she knew she wasn't going to be the one to say no.

The next second Luca pulled back sharply, removing his hands, breaking all contact, leaving her empty and stunned.

"I'm sorry," he said, his voice rough, low. "I have no business touching you. Not like this."

She wanted to yank him back and continue where they left off, but he wasn't hers. This wasn't what they were to each other.

She lowered her gaze and turned just enough to let him know she agreed. That, no, they had no business doing this. Not when she couldn't trust her own judgment.

LUCA GRABBED HIS jacket and got out of the apartment as quickly as he could. What the hell had he done? April was as vulnerable as a newborn kitten. Of course she'd kissed him back. Talk about transference. She was desperate to replace the bitter memories of what Wes had done to her with something tangible, someone who wouldn't steal her money, her dignity.

But he was no better than Wes if he took advantage of her. She needed time to heal. To learn to be on her own, to trust her instincts again. How far had his greed set her back?

The pedestrian traffic on Mott Street was slow. A good thing, as he was barely looking where he was going. The cars were moving faster than earlier, when he'd been with Jillian.

Luca winced.

Goddamn it.

He'd called her April.

Jillian was a smart, beautiful woman. If she never spoke to him again he wouldn't blame her. Because he sure as hell deserved it. Man, he didn't want to think that he'd used her as a substitute for April, or have Jillian think so. But he wasn't so sure that wasn't exactly what he'd done.

He'd gone and fucked up all the way around, hadn't he? He whipped his hair out of his eyes, letting the brisk fall air cool him down.

Jesus, he should have controlled himself better.

He liked April too much to make her feel as though she was being pressured into doing something she didn't want to do. They were stuck in a weird situation and burdened with an imbalance of power. He had most of it, and April had, well, none really. And he'd taken advantage of her by kissing her.

Christ, he wasn't that guy. He couldn't have her thinking he was...

She'd probably be in a rush to leave now, and that

had to be the best thing for both of them. He'd do what he could to help her find a place, even if he had to be sneaky about it. She must've said it a hundred times. She didn't want charity.

Dammit. He was going to miss having her around. He admired her optimism and can-do attitude. Even after what Wes had done.

Most people in her circumstance would've crumbled on the spot. Her resilience was truly admirable. He just hoped his poor judgment hadn't been the thing that finally did her in.

He glanced around, shocked at how far he'd walked in fifteen minutes. He wasn't even in Little Italy anymore. Of course there wasn't a cab in sight, so he turned around and really hustled.

It would serve him right if she was gone before he made it back. He sure as hell hoped she wasn't. He not only owed her a huge apology, he also had to at least try to make things right. Convince her that she had nothing to worry about, at least as far as he was concerned.

FREE Merchandise is 'in the Cards' for you!

Dear Reader,

We're giving away FREE MERCHANDISE!

Seriously, we'd like to reward you for reading this novel by giving you **FREE MERCHANDISE** worth over $20 retail. And no purchase is necessary!

You see the Jack of Hearts sticker above? Paste that sticker in the box on the Free Merchandise Voucher inside. Return the Voucher today... and we'll send you Free Merchandise!

Thanks again for reading one of our novels—and enjoy your Free Merchandise with our compliments!

Pam Powers

Pam Powers

P.S. Look inside to see what Free Merchandise is **"in the cards"** for you!

We'd like to send you two free books like the one you are enjoying now. Your two books have a combined price of over $10 retail, but they are yours to keep absolutely FREE! We'll even send you 2 wonderful surprise gifts. You can't lose!

REMEMBER: Your Free Merchandise, consisting of **2 Free Books** and **2 Free Gifts**, is worth over $20 retail! No purchase is necessary, so please send for your Free Merchandise today.

YOUR FREE MERCHANDISE INCLUDES...
2 FREE Books **AND** 2 FREE Mystery Gifts

FREE MERCHANDISE VOUCHER

2 FREE
BOOKS
and
2 FREE
GIFTS

Please send my Free Merchandise, consisting of
2 Free Books and **2 Free Mystery Gifts**.
I understand that I am under no obligation to buy
anything, as explained on the back of this card.

150/350 HDL GLTM

Please Print

FIRST NAME

LAST NAME

ADDRESS

APT.#   CITY

STATE/PROV.   ZIP/POSTAL CODE

NO PURCHASE NECESSARY!

HB-N16-FMC15

READER SERVICE—Here's how it works:

12

SITTING IMPATIENTLY ON her bed, April heard the front door open and stopped jiggling her foot. Now that Luca was finally back she wasn't sure if she should go downstairs or wait for him to come up. She decided to wait a few minutes. She had the advantage. He couldn't lock her out of his room.

Thinking about how much she'd inconvenienced him made her want to weep. But that wasn't the issue at the moment, so she needed to stay focused on what she wanted to tell him. She thought she heard him on the stairs and she stayed perfectly still. Then she started jiggling her foot again and stopped when Luca appeared in the doorway. He looked terrible.

"Well, I know you didn't have enough time to go on a bender."

"What?" he asked with an adorable frown.

"Never mind. We need to stay on point."

He nodded, but he still looked confused.

"Luca, listen. I appreciate you so much. You letting me stay here and letting me work off some of my debt. Just being great about everything. But I don't think you understand that although I may be in a vulnerable position, *I'm* not vulnerable."

He opened his mouth, but she put up her hand to stop him. "I'm the one who decides what I want to do. Not you. I make my own decisions. Whether good or bad, they're my responsibility."

Luca still looked troubled, although it was a subtle tell that tipped her off. When he felt as if he'd overstepped or gotten something wrong, he developed a little crinkle above his nose. She wanted to smooth those worry lines away, assure him that he had nothing to be concerned about.

"I had no business kissing you," he said. "That was on me. You've been jerked around enough for a lifetime—"

"Stop. Please. I willingly kissed you back. Or did you not notice my participation?"

"Of course I did…" His gaze lingered on her mouth as if he was remembering just how amazing their kiss had been.

"The only thing you should apologize for is running out on me, right when I was getting all revved up. I kissed you back because I liked it. I wanted it. I'd hoped for it."

There were still questions in his eyes, and she couldn't have that. She stood, taking a step toward him. "I'm twenty-six, Luca. A fully grown woman who knows her own mind. Whatever happened between Wes and me has nothing to do with us. We were done for a long time, months before he came out here. He knew it. I knew it. The only problem I foresaw before I arrived was having to sort out the sleeping arrangements, since I knew there was no way I'd get in the same bed as him.

"But I'm very interested in a sexual relationship with

you. Sexual, not romantic, just so we're clear. We have chemistry, which I admit is somewhat inconvenient, but that's the way the cards fell, and I'm pretty sure you agree it's mutual."

Watching his jaw drop and knowing she'd shocked the stuffing out of him, she moved closer and tsked at his buttoned-up shirt. She'd have to do something about that right away, but first, just so he understood exactly what she meant, she put her hand around the nape of his neck and eased him into a kiss.

She wanted it to be clear that she was instigating this time.

Smart man that he was, he got the message loud and clear. His hands went to her back, causing her to flinch involuntarily.

He removed them in a shot, but she shook her head. "Cold, not unwelcome," she said, her mouth so close to his that their lips brushed.

But he didn't press forward. "Are you sure about this?" he asked. "I don't want you to regret anything. We do have a unique situation here."

She had to give him that. Without letting him go, she leaned back, but just a tiny bit. "I'm glad you brought that up. I want you to know that sex won't change anything about how much longer I stay and what I owe you." Something popped into her head that gave her a moment's pause. "I do wish we'd settled on a day you want me out. We've postponed it twice now."

Some of her bravado wavered, but Luca was looking at her intently, which made her feel better.

"How about we agree to revisit the situation next weekend?"

April nodded, trying hard not to show her relief. "And, of course, if I find someplace to live before then,

I'll be out of here. Because I actually do have a promising lead."

"I'm confident we'll work it out."

"Agreed. Now, all you have to do is believe me when I say this is what I want, and I'm not concerned that we'll mistake it for anything other than the fact that we're hot for each other. Okay?"

His answer started with a grin that she'd remember forever, and then a kiss that nearly wiped her memory clean.

He kissed like he worked, thoughtfully, with assurance and a swagger that drove her crazy. When his hands went under her T-shirt again, they were warm as he pulled her close.

She felt his erection pulse when she moved her hips, making her wish they were lying down since he was so much taller.

Breaking the kiss wasn't easy, but there was one more thing. "Wait, please."

His panting was gratifying, so was the fact that he stopped immediately.

"My condoms are in the closet."

"Mine are in my wallet."

He kissed her again, and just as she was getting into a rhythm, he unhooked the back of her bra with one hand.

She returned the favor by tackling his buttons. Thankfully, they were easily undone and by the time she reached his belt, he was already working on removing her shorts.

She tugged his shirt out with both hands, which she also needed for his belt, but she fumbled, and he scratched her behind with his watch band. They both stopped, grinned, took one step back and proceeded to strip themselves.

She already knew what his top half looked like, but she stood rapt as he unzipped then pushed down his pants. He was wearing boxer briefs—navy blue, snug suckers that showed her that he was clearly very enthusiastic about this turn of events.

As he was pushing off his shoes, she couldn't help it—she cupped his erection.

He almost fell but managed to stay on his feet by grabbing on to her hips. "Jesus."

"Sorry. It was just so tempting."

He straightened then picked her up as if she was one of the pillows on her bed. Sliding a hand beneath her knees and another across her back, he kissed her hard and hit the mattress with his knees.

"Ow. Shit. I thought it would be softer."

She couldn't help laughing. "Are you okay?"

"I'm fine. The bruises will be worth it."

She let him set her down. The look in his eyes as he pulled off her T-shirt emboldened her even more. She slipped off her bra and tossed it away.

Luca stood at the foot of the bed, staring as if he was in some sort of trance.

"Uh...how about taking off the rest?"

"Okay," he said. "Just give me a second."

Giggling wasn't something she did. Or hadn't done since she was a teenager, but watching him get rid of his shoes, socks and finally his underwear, had her muffling her laughter behind both hands.

"It's not that funny," he said.

"Uh-huh."

"Come on. Give me a break. I'm normally super-smooth. It's your fault I'm behaving like an idiot."

"My fault?"

He leaned closer. "I've wanted this, too, you know. Since, well, to be honest it started— Never mind."

"What?" she cajoled. "Are you scared I'll make fun of you if you're honest?" She touched his cheek, his skin just barely showing a hint of stubble.

"Something like that," Luca said, laughing. "I will say, after seeing that indomitable spirit of yours I was definitely interested. Can't discount those damn wet T-shirts, though."

She punched his chest gently, but he was so firm she doubted he'd felt it at all. "You're one to talk. I've never known anyone who liked to take his shirt off so much. Jeez. Way to give a girl a heart attack."

"I try," he said. "But first, we need to get you out of these tiny little shorts."

"Think you can handle it?"

"Watch me."

She licked his bottom lip and lay back on the mattress. Then, in another move she wouldn't have thought she had in her, she stretched her arms out like a Victoria's Secret model, and gazed up at him with her best pouty-lipped smile.

It worked. He went slack-jawed again. A moment later he was pulling down her shorts and her panties, his strong hands careful not to tug too hard, even though his impatience was showing.

He leaned back on his knees and looked at her, all spread out for him. She was tempted to cup him again, but she didn't want to break the spell. It felt too delicious, him eating her up with his hungry gaze. Although one peek showed her that he was very ready to move on, the tip of his cock weeping just enough to send a drop sliding down his shaft.

Keeping his eyes on her, he managed to retrieve

the condom. He didn't stop staring as he tore open the packet, but he let his eyes wander downward as he slipped the rubber on over his length, hissing as if it hurt so good.

For once she was grateful they hadn't turned out the lights. Watching him, with that one stray lock of hair falling over his eye, his teeth biting down on his bottom lip as he sheathed himself, was astonishingly arousing—and he wasn't the only one who was wet and ready.

"I feel like I've been waiting for this forever," he said, running his hand down her thigh as he maneuvered himself between her legs. "You are stunning in every way. Look at you. My God."

"You're pretty amazing yourself."

"I'm glad you approve," he said. "But I'm going to stop talking now. I have better things to do with my mouth."

She gasped as he bent forward, took a gentle nip as he passed her belly then spread her open with both thumbs. The first touch of his tongue was aimed so perfectly, she could hardly control herself.

Arching her back, she grabbed a handful of the bottom sheet and slid her other hand into his hair, that gorgeous, soft hair that had tantalized her from the first time she'd seen him.

He hummed as he explored her with his mouth, and when he sucked gently on her swollen clit she felt the vibrations all the way through her body. It was insane to be this turned on so quickly, but then, they'd had several days of foreplay, hadn't they?

His hum turned into a moan—deep, guttural, desperate. A sound that made her writhe under him, wanting him to never stop and wanting him inside her now.

When he started flicking the pointed tip of his tongue, she knew she pulled his hair too hard. But his grunt didn't stop his furious attention. She could feel the wave building, her climax rushing through her like a tsunami. Then he pushed two fingers deep inside her, and she came so hard she nearly bucked him off.

But he didn't let go until her cry came to a gasping end. One moment later he filled her to her limit.

LUCA HAD TO still himself. Close his eyes and take a couple of deep breaths because, holy…she was driving him to an early climax, which he most definitely didn't want.

If he could stretch this moment into a week, he'd do it in a heartbeat, but first, his rapid pulse would have to slow down so he could fully appreciate the woman in his arms.

He opened his eyes once more, and the sight of April still panting, her hair a wild halo on the pillow, her lips moist and parted, was enough to make his cock jerk inside her.

She was gorgeous. So responsive it had been like riding the Coney Island Cyclone, only a thousand times better. His arms trembled as he braced himself above her, their bodies joined perfectly, her right leg slung across his lower back, her left, rubbing against his thigh. More hands were definitely needed, but he had to move. Now.

Slowly, he pulled out until just the tip of his cock was inside her, and damn if she didn't squeeze him hard enough to make him moan. The slide back into her hot, wet silk was the best feeling in the entire world, bar none.

"Oh, babe," she whispered, her head restless as she

stretched her hand to his chest, right over his heart. "You feel amazing."

"Do me a favor," he said. "Don't tell me if this is me hallucinating. This is so much better than I imagined..."

"I know," she said, her eyes widening. "It is, isn't it?" Her voice was wobbly and breathless. "I thought you'd be good, but wow. I'm thinking this could be one of the best decisions ever."

Luca laughed but didn't let it affect his rhythm. He kept moving his hips—sliding his erection out slowly, then plunging it in faster, but not too fast. Pacing was important, but hell, that smile of hers made him want to rush. To get all feral on her and shake the rafters until they were both empty and wrecked.

He bent his arms and stole a kiss from her while he was still filling her up, but when he withdrew it was faster than before, the friction urging him on.

Oh, yes, it was happening. His muscles were tensing in his back, his ass, his legs. He could feel his biceps contract and expand as his breathing grew more urgent.

Thank God he didn't have to worry about neighbors on this floor, because he couldn't be quiet. It surprised him, the loudness of his grunts. He felt like an animal, raw and untamed. Exactly where he belonged.

Soon, she was meeting every thrust; the leg that had been rubbing him had shifted so that her foot was flat on the mattress. Pushing into him, squeezing him as he retreated.

It was the most intense pressure, and the low heat was already beginning deep inside, his balls starting their inexorable climb.

"Too soon," he said, more to himself than to her.

"No," she said, her voice huskier than he remembered. "You're hitting me exactly right. I'm going to come again."

That nearly did him in. He rolled his head, stretched his neck, then thrust into her so hard he moved both their bodies.

"Again," she said, gripping his upper arm with surprising strength.

He grunted as he did as she asked, every muscle straining as he finally crashed into her and then stilled as he came hard enough to make him see white flashes behind his eyes.

At some point he became aware of her voice, her trembling body, the rushing of blood past his ears slowing to a dull roar. And then he could see her. Beautiful, with a flush of pink across her chest and climbing up her neck to fill in her cheeks as if painted by a master.

"I can't," he said, his arms losing their strength. He managed to flop down beside her without breaking any limbs, hers or his.

Together, they sounded like a couple of marathon runners at the 26th mile. Slowly, they came down from their high, finally able to hoard enough air to live another day.

"Holy cow," she said, the grin he couldn't see clear in her voice.

He had the strength to nod, but that was it.

"We probably should have turned down the covers first. I'm starting to get cold, and I don't want to move."

"Well, lucky for you, I'm a certified gent." He ran his hand down her chest, resting it on her perfect breast.

She touched him back, brushing his nipple with the back of her hand. "Uh, I don't think that's going to do the trick," she said.

"Right. Yes." It was difficult, but he hoisted himself

up so he could tug the linens down. She helped a little, lifting her exquisite bottom then raising her legs until he could cover her, goose bumps and all.

"I'll be right back," he said, hating that he had to leave the room, even for the short time it would take him to clean up. But he padded to the bathroom, and before he returned he slung a towel around his waist, hustled downstairs to grab two bottles of water out of the fridge, then hightailed it up the stairs.

He stopped at the bedroom door. It appeared that April had conked out, one hand tucked neatly below her chin. If he'd known, he wouldn't have wasted time getting the water.

"Come on in. I'm not sleeping," she said, although she hadn't opened her eyes. "Despite the fact that you took forever coming back."

"Pardon me for being nice and getting you a bottle of water."

That made her open her eyes. "You're amazing and wonderful, and don't believe anything else you've ever heard."

He grinned, handed her one bottle, put his on the floor then tossed the towel on the floor before climbing in next to her. As soon as she finished taking a huge swig, he rearranged them into a tidy package, her with her head nestled on his chest, him with his arms holding her tightly against him. "Okay?"

"Better than okay."

"If you're really wiped out, it's all right. You can go to sleep."

"Don't want to yet. Actually, we should talk."

"About...?" They'd already talked beforehand. If she was having regrets already...

April ran her hand over his chest and twined her

fingers through his chest hair. It felt so good he relaxed again.

"Please don't think I'm complaining, because I'm not. But the types of things you've had me do, like carrying paint cans that first day, isn't worth a day's rent. Now that I know what it can cost to live in this city, my 'help' isn't even worth fifteen minutes of rent. So, I'm happy to help you do things around the place, but that's all on the house, okay? What I would like is if you had some real projects I could help you with. I think you know by now I really am quite strong and capable."

She looked at him, her brow furrowed just enough to let him know she was serious. He understood where she was coming from, but he didn't like the timing.

As if she could read his mind, she said, "I know. This is something we should've discussed earlier but we didn't, and I just have to make sure we're clear."

"Fine," he said. "We're going to start with the drywall in a few days. You can work with me and Charlie. Good enough?"

She opened her mouth, but instead of an answer, she yawned, which caused him to yawn back.

"Good enough," she said.

Luca rubbed her arm and kissed the top of her head, breathing in the sweet smell that was April. "Now, how about we both get a good night's sleep."

She nodded as she nuzzled his shoulder and whispered, "Tonight was perfect."

He couldn't have agreed more.

13

"WELCOME TO WE CONNECT."

April stopped at the entrance to the theater hosting the Mentor Session of Women Entrepreneurs of New York Tuesday evening and accepted the packet that the volunteer greeter handed her.

"Find a seat anywhere," the woman said. She was a perky sort with short spiked hair and a bolo tie. "I'm Shannon Weeks. You'll find your name tag in your packet. Fill it out like mine—" she pointed to her name, and her business, SuburbanWest, Inc. underneath "—then just network away. Feel free to hand out business cards."

"Thank you, Shannon," April said and entered the room.

The session was free, one of many mentor events where newbies like herself could listen to established business owners, successful women who had started with little more than stubborn determination.

There were at least seventy-five women in the banquet room, running the gamut of ages, all dressed, like her, in casual business attire, most carrying briefcases, also like her, probably containing business plans, biographies, referrals. Basically everything that she could think of that might convince a mentor she would be a perfect mentee.

Everything was set up for networking, and thank goodness April wasn't shy. She went to one of the round tables closest to the podium and selected a seat, and filled out the name tag with her name and As You Wish Concierge Services underneath. When she looked up, a stylish woman who looked to be in her early thirties was putting her briefcase on the chair next to hers.

"I'm April," she said, holding out her hand. "I'm guessing you're involved in the fashion industry?"

The woman laughed as they shook hands. "What gave me away?"

"That fantastic dress." It was a formfitting black sheath underneath a bold floral open kimono cardigan. "It's stunning. Is it your design?"

"Yes, it is. Thank you. I'm Patty Reyes," she said. "It's my third mentoring event."

"My first. I've only been in New York a week."

Patty smiled. "It's really easy to meet people here. This is such a great organization. I already have a mentor. She's a stylist's assistant at *The Today Show*. What are you into?"

April gave her short pitch, and when Patty's eyes lit up, she felt herself relax, at least a little bit.

"I know people who'd sign up for that in a heartbeat."

"Here," April said, pulling a few of her business cards out of her purse. "Feel free to spread them around."

"That pitch of yours is excellent. Just keep doing that. Introducing yourself. Doesn't matter what people's name tags say. We can all help each other. In fact, be sure and look for the blue name tags. Those are mentors willing to help. I'll meet you back here before the talk begins and we'll compare notes. How does that sound?"

"Perfect," she said. "Absolutely perfect."

LUCA WALKED INTO his parents' house while checking his messages. April had just arrived at the Women Entrepreneurs meeting, hoping to make connections and widen her network. All fired up, she was sending him texts every few minutes.

Just met a woman who started her own food truck. She owns five trucks now, and she's a mentor for newbies!

He typed back:

Outstanding! She'll be blown away by you!

"What are you so happy about?"

He looked up to find his brother standing near the dining room table. "What, I can't smile without your permission? Ma didn't tell me you were coming tonight."

"I'm not staying for dinner. Catherine's meeting me in an hour. I just wanted to tell you guys something. Come into the kitchen. I want to tell everyone at the same time."

Luca stopped in front of Tony. "An announcement, huh?"

"Not like that," Tony said. "Not yet, anyway."

They stepped inside the large kitchen. Nothing felt more like home than this spot, with the familiar smells coming from the oven.

"Look, Mom, it's Luca. He hasn't run away."

Luca elbowed his brother in the ribs, then he kissed his mother on the cheek.

"So, you've decided you're still part of the family?" she said.

"Come on. It hasn't been that long. Besides, I knew it was lasagna night, and I couldn't stand having another take-out dinner."

"I left ziti at the office, but Gina said you never came by."

"I heard. That broke my heart. I hope there'll be some leftovers for me to take home tonight."

She smoothed back her salt-and-pepper hair and gave him her Mona Lisa smile, the one that said she'd always have the upper hand.

"Where's Pop?"

"In the basement. Tony," she said. "Go tell him to get up here. He can play with his radio later."

Luca peeked inside the oven to find not only the lasagna, but also an entire pan of her stuffed cabbage. One of his favorite meals. "Ma, you made the Cavolo Ripieno. No wonder I'll never love anyone as much as you."

She waved her spoon at him. "Such nonsense," she said, clearly pleased. "Go help with the table. Dom's coming, too."

"Of course he is, that pig. I have first dibs on the leftovers, right?"

"It's time you started making your own meals. What am I? A chef? I have better things to do."

"Kind of hard when I don't have a stove yet."

"So, maybe you'll come on Sunday and meet Marie Albrogadi. I'm teaching her how to cook. God knows her mother never could make anything except those terrible meatballs."

Luca groaned. Here she went, trying to fix him up again.

"Mom, leave him alone," Tony said. "He just came by to eat and take home some food."

Theresa turned around to Tony. "And has your Catherine asked me even once what your favorite foods are?"

"Stop right there. Dad's coming, and I have something to tell you. And no, I'm not engaged."

"What's the matter?" his father said, closing the basement door behind him. "You love that girl. She loves you. Neither one of you is getting any younger."

"Hey, Pop," Luca said, and his dad clapped him on the back.

The front door opened and slammed shut. Had to be Dom.

"Okay, everyone listen up," Tony began. "Wait. Where's Nonna?"

"Resting. Go ahead and tell us your big announcement."

Just as Dom joined them, Tony said, "We're finishing up Catherine's house and she wants to have all of you over for a celebratory dinner on Saturday."

"But what—"

"Mom, let me finish. She's not trying to take over the family dinners. But she wants to do the cooking," Tony said. Luca hid a smile when he saw his mom's face. "See, this is why I wanted to come talk to you in person." Tony met her glare for glare. "She's been working really hard to impress you, and I want you all to be nice, okay?"

"When are we not nice?" his father said.

Theresa looked hurt. "I wouldn't say a word, but I don't understand why she hasn't asked me about your favorite meals. I could help teach her."

"That's the whole point," Tony said. "She wants to

show you that she's paid attention. Okay? Just, please. It's important to me."

"I'm in," Dom said. "Anyone who cooks for me is A-okay in my book."

Luca shook his head as he turned to his younger brother, who looked as if he'd just stepped out of *GQ* magazine. His expensive suit had been tailored. Ten-to-one odds he had a date after dinner. Someone uptown. "You have a whole stable of women making you meals and giving you free donuts and God knows what else. And just so you know, tonight I get all the leftovers, *capisci*?"

"The hell you will. I've got to keep up my strength with all the work I'm doing for the company."

"Oh, like what? Combing your hair five times a day? Flirting all over town?"

"Shut up."

"All of you," their mom said, "out of my kitchen. Dinner is in twenty minutes. Get the table ready. Tony, did you open the wine?"

"Right when I got here," he said and led his brothers into the dining room while their father went to the old stereo in the living room where he kept his collection of LPs. A moment later Dean Martin was singing something sentimental about Italy.

"I'll be right there," Luca said, pulling his cell phone out of his pocket. It was April, of course. Still excited if the exclamation marks were anything to go by.

OMG! Elena, the woman with the food trucks, has agreed to be my mentor! And she's going to introduce me to some of the microlenders that are here tonight. This is the best thing in the whole world!

"Hey," Dom said. "Aren't you the one who's always telling me to put my phone away?"

Ignoring him, Luca smiled at the text.

Tony looked at him. "You're in a good mood. I guess that date paid off."

"Oh, right," Dom said. "You gonna bring that hottie you've been seeing to meet the family?"

"What are you talking about?" Luca asked.

"What? You didn't think Charlie or Scott would tell us about her?"

Luca shook his head. How could he have forgotten? Of course none of those guys would keep their goddamn mouths shut.

"Hey, I didn't hear anything." Tony looked at Luca. "Are you talking about the woman from Columbia?"

"Her name's April," Dom said, butting in before sitting down at the other side of the long table.

Luca took a deep breath. This wasn't a bad thing, Dom mentioning April. Maybe his mother and grandmother would quit trying to find him a wife. "Yes," he said. "I'm seeing a woman named April."

"Wait a minute." Their mom had been in the kitchen but she'd suddenly materialized and was all ears. "This is someone serious?"

"Not sure yet. I like her a lot, though."

"But you didn't bring her to dinner?"

"She's working tonight. I'll ask her to come with me to Catherine's on Saturday."

"That's some fast maneuvering," Tony said in a low voice after their mom started back to the kitchen. "You haven't even been out of the house two weeks."

"Look who's talking. You were crazy about Catherine right off the bat."

Tony grinned. "True. Well, good. Can't wait to meet her."

"She might say no, so don't get too excited."

Dom moved over to the table they used to set out the dessert and wine. "I just hope for your sake April's Italian," he murmured so only Luca could hear.

"What about Marie Albrogadi?" Theresa asked, coming back into the dining room.

"Her mother makes terrible meatballs," Luca said. "Marie probably does, too."

Everyone laughed, even his mom.

"And why isn't the table set?" she asked.

"Got it," Luca said, going for the plates.

Tony headed for the silver.

Dom poured himself a glass of wine.

Their mother had turned to go back to the kitchen, but first she looked at Luca again. "April? I don't recall there being a Saint April."

Luca closed his eyes. "I'm not marrying her, Ma. Okay? She's a nice girl from St. Louis and she doesn't know a lot of people in New York."

His mother shook her head as she walked back to the stove. "So you couldn't find an Italian stranger?"

14

It was just past 6:00 p.m. when April escaped the over-crowded subway. The evening was settling in, and she couldn't wait to get back to the apartment. Maybe Luca would be there? She'd gotten home so late last night that he'd already been asleep, and tempting as it was, she hadn't had the heart to wake him.

There were enough pedestrians to make walking the two blocks to Luca's an adventure, so she moved in closer to the shops. Man, she loved this street. Actually, she was crazy about the whole neighborhood, and she hated the idea that she couldn't afford to live anywhere near there.

Instead of dwelling on it, she focused on the wares in the windows as she passed. Electronics didn't thrill her so much, and she didn't need any suitcases. But there was a store that specialized in leather handbags and featured an Italian leather, dark blue folio for four hundred dollars that was exactly her taste. Too rich for her blood, but last week when she'd stopped to drool over it, she'd met Mrs. Brivio who owned the resale shop next door. It had quickly become April's favorite place to browse. To her delight, Mrs. Brivio happened to be standing at the entrance.

"Hello, April."

"Good evening," she said, so glad they'd gotten to know each other a little. "How are you today?"

The woman shrugged her shawl-covered shoulders. "I'm cold and it's not even winter. Why do I keep living in this city?"

"Because it's magical?"

"You're new here. Give it a few years."

"I would love to. Any chance someone suddenly decided to rent out their apartment?"

Mrs. B. laughed. "You mean since you asked two days ago?" she said, just as a woman April hadn't seen before joined them. "Val, have you heard of any places for rent right now?"

"Around here?" Val was closer to April's age and absolutely striking. Her long dark hair was pulled back into a French braid, and she wore a beautiful rust-colored midi skirt topped with a matching fitted jacket. "Not likely." She gave April a sympathetic smile. "I know of a few co-ops for sale."

"I can only imagine how much those cost," April said.

"Outsiders have been willing to pay outrageous prices for them, so I really can't blame the young people who inherit and sell. They couldn't get enough rent money to justify holding on to them."

"Really? Because I've been looking and even tiny studio apartments go for about fifteen hundred."

"No kidding." Val looked at Mrs. B. "I can't think of anyone I know who pays more than five or six hundred for a two-bedroom around here, can you?"

Mrs. B shook her head. "The rent increases have

been next to nothing for the last thirty years. That's why no one leaves."

April nodded, trying not to deflate completely. "Rent control?"

"No," Mrs. B said, frowning. "I don't know how it works, exactly, but we've been here so long, we don't ask. I think we're all afraid if we say anything the rents will go up."

"Where can I sign up for that?"

To April's great dismay, both women chuckled. "It doesn't work that way, sweetheart," Mrs. Brivio said. "I'm sorry. Have you met Val De Vitis? She lives two doors down. Her husband is a stock trader on Wall Street. Her grandfather used to make violins. Beautiful, beautiful work."

A piercing whistle came from the street, followed by a man's voice calling out, "Hey, April. April, over here."

She reluctantly turned, hoping it wasn't Vinny.

Luca had just gotten out of a white truck and was headed toward her, but it wasn't Luca who had called her name. Luca turned and said something to the driver, who looked familiar...

Wait. Was that Charlie? The guy who'd brought up Luca's recliner? Well, whoever he was, he was laughing at Luca's not-so-discreet hand gesture.

Honking got the truck moving, and she waited as Luca maneuvered his way between pedestrians, heading toward her.

"You know the Paladinos?" Val said.

"I know Luca, lucky me."

"April is new to New York," Mrs. Brivio said just as he walked up to them. "She's got family in Positano."

"That's a beautiful city." Val turned to Luca, who

had a very surprised look on his face. "Your family is from the coast, yes?"

He nodded. "Naples."

"Ours, too, but if I remember correctly, not from the same neighborhood."

"My mother would know," he said.

"And how is your family? I heard your father wasn't well."

April was aware that he answered but she was too busy staring at his perfect mouth to follow the conversation. And remembering exactly what he could do with that mouth was about to get her in trouble. She wondered what Luca would do if she attacked him right there, right then. This was New York, after all. No one would bat an eye.

Sensing a sudden lull, she pulled herself out of her silly daydream to rejoin the conversation. Better yet, she should grab Luca and make a beeline to the apartment and ravage him. The thought made her smile.

The two women smiled back.

April cleared her throat. "I should be on my way," she said. "Very nice to meet you, Val. I hope to see you again soon. And Mrs. Brivio, remember to—"

"If I hear of a place for rent I'll let you know," she said, laughing.

April turned to Luca then hesitated, carefully choosing her words since their living arrangement was no one's business. "Are you headed home?"

His smile might have given away that they were more than just friends. "Come on, I'll walk with you."

They'd barely blended in with the pedestrian traffic when Luca said, "You have family in Italy?"

"Yes. I thought I'd said."

"You're kidding? Branagan? I never would have guessed."

"That's because it's my mom's family."

"Huh. So do you speak any Italian?"

"Not much, but I understand it pretty well. Nonna's English isn't all that great so I— What?" April laughed at his goofy grin. "*Nonna* means grandmother."

"I know what it means," Luca said. "It just sounded strange coming from you."

"My middle name is Michela, after her. Do you speak Italian?"

"Like you, I mostly understand it, but I can string a few sentences together. And curse words, I know all of them."

April grinned. "Me, too."

They'd slowed down, annoying people who were rushing to get around them. Her hip brushed Luca's leg, and then someone cut her off and she stumbled against him.

He put a hand on her back. "Are you okay?"

"This is when I hate being short the most. Big crowds make me feel claustrophobic."

Luca frowned. "You must despise the subway," he said, sliding his arm around her and pulling her against his body as if she belonged there.

"I usually wait for everyone to get off ahead of me. I found out something interesting. There are apartments in this neighborhood going for less than six hundred bucks a month."

Luca tensed. She felt it in his arm, his whole body. "Is that what those women told you?"

"I don't know if it was Mrs. B. or Val, but they both knew about it. I don't think they meant a few here and there, either. And it's not rent control, because I asked."

"No, it's not rent control," he said with a thoughtful frown. "What did they say it was?"

"They weren't really sure how it worked. And they don't want to make waves asking about it. I can't blame them for that."

Two men paying no attention to where they were going bumped into them. Luca's arm fell away and she wanted to give the rude hipster in a tight blue suit a swift kick in the pants. Although now she was able to see Luca's face better and something was definitely bothering him.

He barely spared the men a glance.

"There are places where the rent is inexpensive, both business and residential units, but they're connected to old families that have lived in Little Italy for generations. It has to do with papers the first wave of immigrants signed when they came over. Private agreements."

"Well, does that mean no one ever moves? A kid could go off to college and a room could become available, no?"

His frown deepened. There was the telltale crinkle over his nose. Did he not want her to live too close to him? The thought hurt.

"I wouldn't cramp your style, you know."

"No," he said, reaching for her hand. "It's not that. I just don't want you to get your hopes up. It hardly ever happens. These families hold on to those rentals like they're pure gold. If I knew different, of course I would've told you."

"I know," she said, squeezing his hand. She was disappointed, although it made sense there had to be a special reason for anyone in New York to live that cheaply. "Anyway, I'm going to be meeting up with Grace, a friend I made at that silent auction, and there's a good chance her roommate is moving to California. So that's my best bet at the moment."

"Where's the apartment?"

"Perth Amboy. It's in New—"

"I know exactly where that is," he said, giving her a long look. "It's far."

"Yep." She shrugged. "C'est la vie."

He seemed puzzled, though she doubted he thought their having sex had changed anything. She still needed to find her own place, prove she could make it on her own. In fact, she was all the more determined to move out as soon as possible. It was already hard to imagine not waking up with Luca and seeing him every evening. And it was bound to get worse because her feelings for him were starting to shift. But if there was going to be more between them than no-strings sex, it couldn't happen unless they had separate lives. Their relationship needed room to grow. Or wither away. She needed to be prepared for both outcomes.

Brave thoughts. When he pulled her closer and put his arm around her shoulders again, she wanted to weep with relief.

"I want to hear about this mentor you found at your meeting. And why you didn't wake me last night like you were supposed to." He leaned in close, so his mouth brushed her ear. "But first, I've got a surprise for you."

"What?"

"Patience," he said as they stopped at the corner for traffic. "See that drugstore?" He pointed out what looked like a store that had been around for a long time. "There used to be a candy counter in the front, near the door. When I was nine I stole a piece of candy. It wasn't like a chocolate bar or anything, it was just a sour ball."

"Naughty."

"Yeah, well, my life of crime was short-lived. Even though the owner, who was a nice old man named Giuseppe, didn't see me, someone else from the neighborhood did. Now, my parents' house isn't all that close. They live on the other side of old Little Italy. But by the time I got home, my mother knew all about my petty thievery, my father was called from his office to come deal with me and I was marched back to the store, a bunch of neighbors trailing after us."

"Oh, you poor thing."

"It was mortifying. I had to apologize then work off the price of the candy, which was two days' worth of helping Giuseppe clean the front window and dusting every shelf in the store, a far greater penalty than the crime warranted."

"But I bet you never stole anything again."

"I did not," he said, slowing his step in front of Giuseppe's 5 & Dime, a fondness in his smile. "His granddaughter runs the place now."

"You know what?" April said as they moved on, turning left instead of right. She loved the feeling of his arm around her shoulders, and if it wasn't for the promise of what came next, she'd have liked to walk all over Little Italy just like this.

"What?"

"Even if I don't get to live here, I'm still glad I know the neighborhood a little. It reminds me of home, believe it or not. Even though it's part of big, bad New York City, it has a small-town flavor I like a lot."

"There's a lot to like. Although, it has its drawbacks, too. The gossip and rumors that fly around here… Hell, me with my arm around your shoulders? That'll be all over every church within five miles by Sunday."

"I wondered about that," she said. "If you cared about what Mrs. B. or Val or anyone else thought about, well, you know…you, me. Whatever…"

"Obviously I don't. You okay with this?"

"Totally okay."

He picked up the pace until they got to an old building. There was a garage at street level with a heavy-duty lock securing the wide pull-down door. Luca pulled out a key and a moment later they stepped inside. He flipped three light switches and the whole place came to life.

The first thing she saw was his motorcycle. Spit-polish shiny, sparkling chrome and pristine leather. "Wow. Nice."

"You're the only person I've ever brought here."

"Really? What about your brothers?"

"Dom and my folks know I have a bike but I've never told them where I keep it. Only Tony knows I have a workshop, but he hasn't seen it."

"I'm very honored." She moved close enough to the bike to run her hand across the seat as she looked around the huge space. The bike rested on a big mat, but the rest of the floor was Plexiglas tile. Three quarters of the space was taken up by a workshop that made her father's setup look like child's play. Behind her, Luca pulled down the door then came up next to her.

"Come on," he said, taking her hand. "I'll show you around."

He walked her to the nearest wall and started pointing from the middle out. "Main workbench, table saw and dust collector, router table, band saw—"

She already knew what most of the equipment was, although his was certainly top-notch. Her real interest was Luca himself, the change in him as he talked.

There'd been glimpses of this side of him at the apartment. No wonder this was his happy place. His love for his work and his tools was written in the smile lines by his eyes, the way he squeezed her hand. This place was the spark that lit Luca's inner fire.

"Does this have anything to do with your job?"

"I do quite a bit of finish work for the company, but nope, this is for me."

When she saw the king-size carved headboard against the far wall, she gasped. The piece was exquisite. Dark cherrywood with simple square designs, it had Luca's stamp all over it. How easily she could imagine him here, at the bench, working with his hands on each tiny detail until it was exactly the way he wanted it. "I sure hope you're keeping that gorgeous headboard for yourself."

He nodded and gestured to the corner. "I've started on a dresser out of the same wood, but first, I have to finish a coffee table for a client."

She glanced at the other partially finished pieces he had lying about. "I don't even know what to say. Everything is so— God, Luca, I can really picture you here. Creating. Designing each unique piece. Not bending over a set of blueprints—" She stopped, immediately regretting her words. How dare she judge his chosen profession.

Luca looked into her eyes as if she'd surprised him, but he didn't seem the least bit angry.

"I'm so glad you brought me here," she said, slipping her hand from his hold, but only so she could cup his nape and bring him into a kiss.

Once she'd touched his lips with her own, things got urgent fast. She ran one hand through his hair while skimming the other down his back, loving the feel of his muscles bunching beneath her palm.

BY THE TIME he'd slipped her jacket off her shoulders and pulled her blouse out from her skirt, April had undone his belt and started wrestling his shirt up with both hands. He'd thought briefly about taking her back to the apartment, but there was no way he wasn't going to have her in this room. Right now.

Kissing her again eased a part of him that he hadn't realized was tense. Her eager response was making him harder by the second. The way things were going, he'd probably lose it before he figured out just how he was going to manage all he wanted to do with her.

He slipped a condom out of his wallet while he still had his wits about him and she grinned up at him. After handing the packet to her, he lifted her straight up into his arms and she slipped her legs around his waist as if they'd rehearsed the move a dozen times. He somehow got them pointed in the right direction, still kissing and panting as if they'd run up four flights of stairs.

April briefly looked up. "Where are we going?"

"Wall."

"Brilliant." She kissed him as if the brief interruption had never happened. He shifted her body in his arms, boosting her a little higher so he could get a firmer grip. She wasn't heavy but his fingers were digging too hard into her sweet behind.

After rushing the last few steps, he got her braced against the wall between the workshop and where he parked his bike. She nearly took them both down with her constant squirming, determined to find the perfect angle for their mouths. He tightened his hold until she was satisfied.

"You should've woken me up last night," he said before leaning in again to take her mouth, making absolutely sure she understood there was nothing in the world that he wanted more than her at this moment.

The way she moaned nearly threw him off balance, but he managed to stay on his feet as he used one hand to undo the buttons on the front of her dressy blouse.

She returned the favor by pulling down his zipper and pushing his pants and his boxer briefs down as far as she could reach. He did the rest.

"You're going too slow," she said, squeezing him hard with her legs, and damn if she didn't maneuver her skirt up around her waist. Relaxing those incredible thigh muscles, her hand went around his cock. "You're going to have to do something about my panties."

"I always want to do something about your panties."

She laughed and circled her thumb over the head of his very erect cock.

"Slow down, woman. You're going to end this before we've begun."

"That's okay," she said, pumping him slowly as he unfastened the front clasp of her bra. "It's early. We can go again back at your place."

He thrust his tongue between her lips and slipped the crotch of her panties to the side. She pinched his nipple, almost making him come before he was ready. "That was a nice little squeak there, big guy," she said, her lips inches from his.

"You're playing with fire. You know that, right?"

"I know exactly what I'm doing," she whispered before her lips brushed his.

Up for the challenge, he swiped her bottom lip with his tongue, then in one smooth move, raised her whole body up until he had her nipple between his teeth.

Talk about squeaking. He grinned, not letting her

go, pointed his tongue and began flicking just the tip of her beautiful beaded nipple.

The squeak turned into a groan, and his arms started shaking so hard he had to lower her. She firmly locked her legs behind his back. Miraculously, she still had the condom packet in her left hand, and she ripped it open before unfurling it down his hard length.

He moaned as if she was killing him, but then there was nothing stopping him from his main objective. Trembling, he got her into the perfect position and thrust inside her.

They both groaned, and her forehead dropped to his shoulder while he bit his lower lip so he wouldn't lose it right that second. About a dozen rapid heartbeats later, he started to move.

And she started squeezing his cock.

It wasn't elegant at all. But it was scorching hot. Especially when he got his right hand between them, his thumb on her clit, his movements creating just the right amount of friction. She actually climaxed seconds before him, which was everything he could have wanted.

By the time he let her down, his legs were wobbly, his breathing labored, and he figured a heart attack wasn't completely out of the question.

April wasn't doing much better. In fact, it was a good thing they weren't far from the apartment because he figured he might just have to carry her.

15

EVENTUALLY, THEY RECOVERED enough to walk home. Once in the elevator, she leaned back against him. "Oh, my God. That was amazing."

"Yeah." Luca's breath on her cheek made her melt inside. "You're gorgeous, you know that?"

"Thank you. You're not so bad yourself." She could actually feel his slow grin as he nuzzled her neck. When they got to his floor, she straightened. "Will you take me for a ride on your Harley sometime?"

"Of course I will. Anytime." As he unlocked the front door, he said, "Hey, are you working this Saturday night?"

"I think so."

"When will you know for sure?"

"Maybe tomorrow. Why?"

"I know those events are good money, but any chance I could convince you to go someplace with me?"

"Of course," she said, careful not to sound too eager.

"Great. There's this family dinner thing at my brother's girlfriend's house. I'd like it if you'd come with me."

"I'd be happy to." That she hadn't expected. "When

you say family dinner, it's not just your brothers, but your parents, too?"

"Yep. And Nonna," he said, reaching for her hand. "Listen, I know I'm asking a lot of you to give up an event, so I'll make it a bonus night."

"A what?"

"To be honest, there'll be some interrogation involved, nothing too scary, but it's only fair I give you triple." Luca must've noticed her confusion. "You know, credit against your rent tab. I'm not trying to pull anything over on you. It's not charity. I think I told you about how my mom and nonna are always trying to set me up. After meeting you they should ease up for a while."

The butterflies in her stomach had frozen, as had her smile. This was just another trade-off. She wasn't going with him as a real date. Which shouldn't have been as devastating as it was. She knew the score. Hell, she'd made the rules. But for a moment there, she'd let her imagination run free. The idea of really being his date and meeting his family had thrilled her. Made her forget who and what they really were to each other. That was why she needed to move out, and quickly.

She cleared her throat, not wanting to reveal her reaction. "I'll do my best to help. You'll have to prep me, though."

He shook his head. "All I told them was that I was seeing someone, and I wanted to see where it would go. We should probably give them the impression we're exclusive."

"Sure, that makes sense."

"You'll like Catherine. She works at the UN. And she's cooking the whole dinner, which is a big deal. Italian food. Which is my mother's territory. Which reminds me, I brought home leftovers from the other night."

"I saw that."

"You hungry?"

"Starved." At least she had been a few minutes ago. She followed him to the kitchen.

"How about I put some lasagna in the microwave?"

"That sounds great, thanks." It would be a huge mistake to think of the two of them as a real couple. She knew that. Would they even be sleeping with each other if she'd already moved out?

There was no doubt in her mind that Luca liked her. But that didn't mean she was anything more than a convenience to him. The attraction was real, yes, but it was only that. A physical attraction. On her part, too.

Right? Was that all it was? Had she let his kindness fool her into thinking he was more than a friend with benefits?

She was fully prepared to create a business on her own, to find a place to live in the most expensive city she could imagine, to pay off her debts and be solely responsible for her future. And yet, when it came to Luca, she wasn't quite so confident.

If she was going to continue to sleep with him while living under his roof, she'd have to be absolutely sure not to trick herself into thinking they were in a relationship. The last thing she needed was to let her heart fill up with impossible expectations.

The quickest way to remind herself to knock it off was to think of Wes.

His name alone made her shudder.

"Should we set up the card table?" Luca asked. "Or do you want to eat in the bedroom?"

They both knew what eating in bed would lead to.

"I'll set up the table," she said, refusing to look for his reaction.

She pulled out the folding chairs, disturbing the rolled-up blueprints he'd stashed behind them. They fell over and she picked them up and leaned the rolls against the wall.

"Why do you want to be an architect?" she asked.

Luca laughed. "Where did that come from?" His gaze lowered to the blueprints. "I told you the other day."

"Actually, you told me how you being licensed would help your family business get more jobs."

Shrugging, he turned away to put the two plates of lasagna in the microwave. "Same thing."

"Not really. It's kind of hard to imagine you getting excited over building chain stores or public housing. Especially after seeing your amazing carpentry work." She saw part of a resigned smile before he opened the fridge.

He brought out a couple of beers and handed one to her but said nothing.

April bit her lip. It was important to remember that Luca had a life here and his own priorities. Just because they were sleeping together didn't make his job any of her business.

Still, the tightness in her stomach wouldn't go away. She might not have known him a long time, but she could see where his heart lay when it came to his professional life. But it also made sense that he would set his personal desires aside in order to help his family.

Her phone signaled a text. She glanced at it and couldn't be more grateful. "Hey, do I have time to make a call?"

"Sure, the lasagna won't be ready for about seven minutes."

"I'll be quick. My friend Grace just texted me about that apartment in Perth Amboy. Wish me luck," she called behind her as she raced up the stairs.

"SHIT." LUCA STARED at the food going around in the microwave. He had the same reaction to her moving to Jersey as he'd had the other day. Moving to Perth Amboy was the first step to her going back to St. Louis. She'd hate it there. The commute would be unbearable. She'd quickly figure out that Jersey wasn't all that much cheaper than New York. It would make her old hometown seem like a comfortable and sane alternative.

He pulled his phone out of his pocket and hit speed dial. He hadn't wanted to do this but...

Tony answered right away. "Hey, what's up?"

"I wanted to let you and Catherine know that April is coming with me on Saturday."

"Good. I look forward to meeting her."

"Yeah, she's great. Mom and Nonna should like her. Hopefully this'll make them leave me alone for a while."

"Ah." Tony paused. "Is that the only reason you're bringing her? Is there even anything going on between you two?"

"Yeah, sort of." Luca walked over to make sure April wasn't coming down the stairs. "I like her a lot. She's responsible, ambitious, works hard even though she's had a tough time. I think I mentioned she's new to the city and she's had a rocky start trying to get her business up and running. Having a long commute to Jersey might be the final straw. Although she's very determined..." Luca couldn't help smiling. "She's got the kind of attitude that makes you root for her, you know what I mean?"

"Huh. I haven't heard you talk about a woman like

that in a long time," Tony said. "Scratch that. You've never talked about a woman like that."

Luca wished he'd curbed his enthusiasm, at least a little. He didn't want anyone getting the wrong idea. On the other hand… "Hey, let me ask you something." He lowered his voice. "How much have you told Catherine about the Trust?"

"The Trust? Uh, everything now. But that's because she's going to be part of the family. Why? Are you and April that serious?"

"No, it's not like that."

"That's good, because I think Mom would have a stroke, you getting serious with another non-Italian so soon after me."

"She's actually half Italian, on her mother's side. But look, here's what I need to know. Is that one-bedroom still vacant in the Hester Street building?"

"I think so, but I'd have to check."

"If it is, would it be possible to rent it out to April without violating the terms of the Trust? I mean, you're the executor now, since Dad passed on the business, so what do you think?"

Tony was silent for a few seconds. "Things have changed so much since the original language in the Trust, and it hasn't been updated since before the gentrification began. We really need to take a new look at the whole thing, see how we can make it more relevant for the neighborhood as it is. That being said, I can't see a reason why we couldn't justify renting to April."

"I don't want anyone getting bent out of shape over it. If we need to, I'll subsidize the rent, although if we do this, she can't know I had anything to do with it."

"How are you going to explain the price?"

"I'll figure it out. She's talked to some of the merchants and knows something is going on with controlled rents in the neighborhood, so I can use that."

"What's being said? Anything I should know about?"

"No." Luca heard the microwave beep. "Nothing new. Nobody wants to make waves."

"Good."

"You want me to mention this to Pop?"

"I don't see the point. Mom doesn't want us involving him in the business. Same with the Trust. It's not like we're doing anything wrong or illegal. It's all Paladino money and property." Tony paused. "Although I'd like to hear you explain to him how *it's not like that* with April."

"Shut up."

Tony laughed. "Look, I'm going to tell you something because I feel that I should," he said, his tone serious. "And before you jump down my throat, I'm only going to say this once. Two weeks ago you told me you were looking forward to being on your own, that you wanted time to yourself, to be able to bring a woman home if you wanted. You haven't had much time or personal space yet. So, I guess I'm just saying, be careful about jumping into anything too fast."

Luca frowned, feeling some attitude creep in. Hell, he knew his brother had a point, but Tony didn't understand the circumstances and Luca didn't want to talk about it. He and April had something, a connection that was growing stronger every day. The last thing he wanted was for her to move hours away. If she had a huge commute, they'd hardly see each other.

"Grace's roommate took the job," April called out as she bounced down the stairs. "But I have to wait a week to see the place."

Luca covered the phone. "Look, I've got to go but

can you get back to me pretty quick?" he asked, then disconnected the moment he heard Tony say, "Sure."

THREE DAYS LATER the yellow cab turned the corner of Catherine's block. Luca was looking forward to getting his first look inside the finished interior.

He watched April's reaction as her gaze caught on the beautiful stained glass, art deco front door, her eyes widening in appreciation. "Wow," she said, her voice as reverent as a church whisper. "Did you do any of that?"

"No, Tony handled everything. I think I said, but that's how he and Catherine met." He paid the cabbie and they got out.

Damn. It was killing him not to tell April about the Hester Street apartment. Tony had called yesterday. Luca couldn't risk her bringing it up at dinner, so he was waiting to surprise her later, after they'd left.

"All right." April took a deep breath, not moving from the curb. "Um, one more time, please? Tony's the oldest, and he runs Paladino & Sons ever since your father had his second heart attack. Your mother prides herself in her cooking, but I should still feel free to compliment Catherine although not go overboard. Dom is the youngest, and he's something of a ladies' man and flirts with everyone so don't pay any attention to him. And are you sure I look all right?"

For the first time since he'd asked her to dinner, April sounded nervous. "You look beautiful. That dress is perfect. I'm not sure how you're able to walk in those heels, but they look great."

"Thank you," she said, holding on tight to her clutch. "Oh, and Nonna speaks mostly Italian, and your father—"

"Quit worrying," he said, teasing one hand away from

her death grip on the purse so he could give it a reassuring squeeze. He hadn't felt the need to prep her, but she'd insisted. April was outgoing and always upbeat—he hadn't imagined this would be hard for her at all. "They're nice people, I promise. But be warned. If you mention that you're half Italian, my mother will have the church booked before dessert."

April smiled. "Okay, I'll keep that quiet."

"You've got nothing to worry about." He gave her a one-armed hug before guiding her toward the porch. "I'm hoping you'll have a good time this evening."

"Oh, I will." She stopped and faced him. "I'm sure of it. It's just…well, this is important. I really want to be the kind of woman your family can picture you being with…" She blushed and lifted her shoulders in a small shrug. "Otherwise your mom and nonna will keep pestering you."

"Is that all that's making you nervous?"

She nodded, her gaze steady and solemn.

"I wish you would've said something." Luca smiled and touched her cheek. "All that worry for nothing. You're exactly the type of woman they'd want for me."

April gave him a surprisingly shy smile. Her cheeks and lips were pink, and he figured he might just have to kiss her right there on the sidewalk.

Luca leaned forward as Tony opened the front door.

"Hey," Tony said with a wry laugh. "Want me to come back?"

"Thanks, bro. Great timing." Luca looked at April, hoping she wasn't embarrassed.

She seemed fine, smiling at Tony as he opened the door wider and welcomed them into the beautiful foyer. Catherine joined them, and introductions were made.

"Come on," Tony said. "Let me give you a quick tour, huh?"

"I'll meet you down here when you're done," Catherine said, taking the bottle of chilled Prosecco that Luca had brought. "I've got to check the—" She waved in the general direction of the kitchen then disappeared.

From the staircase and the restored fireplaces, to the deco inlays and details on everything from the windows to the light switches, there wasn't one misstep. Luca could see how much Tony enjoyed showing April all the little touches, watching as her eyes widened with wonder.

"Man, this is one of the best things you've ever done. I mean it," Luca said as his brother showed them the new electric dumbwaiter.

"I have to admit," Tony said, "I had no idea how much I missed the actual art of restoration. How amazing it is to look to the past instead of just the new and modern. The craftsmanship was remarkable back in the 30s and 40s. Look at that tile. The glass work."

"Have you taken pictures of the detail work?" Luca asked. "If Catherine doesn't mind, this should all be showcased in the new brochure Dom's working on."

"Huh." Tony swept a considering gaze around the room. "You're right. I think we might get some interest in more restoration work with it."

"Definitely." Luca nodded. "Not everybody's got the touch, though. We get too many of these types of jobs and you might have to get back out in the field."

"I'd have no problem with that," Tony said, and Luca thought of how great it was to hear the pride in his brother's voice.

"Well, obviously I know nothing about any of this

except that it's all stunning," April said. "Yet it still feels warm and comfortable in here."

"Repeat that to Catherine, will you?" Tony asked. "She'll like that. It's what she was hoping for."

"Did she help you do all this?" April's eyes were just as wide as they were when they started the tour of the house.

"A lot of it, yes."

It shouldn't have mattered to Luca but he was pleased that April had an appreciation for the work, even the small details most people would miss. She'd asked lots of questions and wanted to see every nook and cranny.

Finally they arrived at the new chef's kitchen, and Luca grinned at April's reaction. The throaty moan had Catherine glancing over her shoulder.

"Totally swoon-worthy." April was trying to look everywhere at once.

"I can see you meant that literally," Catherine said with a laugh.

"Oh, I was making noises, huh? Wow, you've got so many things going on in here. How can I help?"

Catherine's grin was equal parts relieved and panicked. "I'll get you an apron."

"Come on," Tony said, nodding at Luca. "Let's go open the rest of the wine."

Luca followed him to the large dining room. The table looked like something out of a magazine, complete with an elegant centerpiece and enough wineglasses to make him glad they were going to take a cab home. "Don't take this the wrong way, but I didn't know you had this in you. I've been so used to seeing you behind total remodels."

"What can I say? Catherine inspired me. Now pour

me some of that Prosecco." He shot a glan̶c̶ kitchen. "By the way, have you told her yet?

Luca shook his head. "Tonight. After we get h̶

Tony's slight frown made Luca realize how muc̶ h̶ he'd just told his brother about his relationship with April.

"We're calling it an open-ended sublet," Tony said, lowering his voice. "I made sure Francis knows we're helping a friend out. If April asks anything, he's supposed to tell her that a tenant named Robert DeLaria is working in Rome indefinitely but he didn't want to let the place go." He took a sip. "Something just occurred to me. You want me to have some of the furniture from the warehouse put in? You know…since it's supposed to be a sublet."

Luca sighed, glad one of them was thinking straight. "You're right, we should. Thanks."

"I doubt there's much to choose from so it won't be anything special. Just a bed, a table, couch, those kinds of things. It'll have to wait until Monday."

"I owe you."

"Damn right. Tell you what… Finish your internship and we'll call it even."

Luca's gut tightened.

Tony grinned. "Now tell me more about April."

16

APRIL HADN'T PICTURED Catherine being so pretty. Blonde, with dark blue eyes, she was tall and held herself with an air of confidence April admired. It helped that she seemed extremely grateful for the company and the assistance. "Your sauce smells amazing," April said.

"Thanks. Would you mind giving it a taste? If you've ever had his mother's food, you'd understand why I'm so nervous about mine."

April had eaten the leftovers Luca had brought home and they had been really good. But she decided not to mention anything that might reveal her and Luca's living arrangements.

Catherine got out a spoon as they went to the big six-burner stove. After taking another good whiff of the sauce when the cover came off the pot, April felt sure Catherine was in the ballpark. "Oh," she said, letting the flavor bloom in her mouth. "It's so, so good."

"But…?" Catherine's look was pleading.

"You have nothing to worry about. Seriously, it's excellent."

Catherine sighed with relief and smiled at April. "So, you're from St. Louis, right?"

April nodded. "New York has been qui⟨...⟩
ment. But Luca's been great. Other than Tony, ⟨...⟩
met any of the Paladinos before. Did you get along ⟨...⟩
them right away?"

"Um, not really," Catherine said, checking the stuffed
porchetta in the oven. "I'm not Italian, for one thing, but
they really are good people. They've got their ways, but
I'm sure if Luca thinks you're special, which he obviously does, then they will, too."

April thought about what Luca had said just before
Tony opened the door. It should've helped her relax, not
had the opposite effect. That his parents would think
she was a woman who would be good for Luca wasn't at
all the same as her being someone Luca would choose
for himself. Not that it had any bearing on today or
this dinner.

"There's no chance I'm going to relax, but thanks
for the pep talk. Meeting parents is always terrifying,
no matter what the circumstances."

Catherine lifted her water glass. "Amen to that," she
said and was cut off by the doorbell. "Hell, we should've
been drinking wine all this time."

They both laughed. Then lucky Catherine got to stay
in the kitchen to keep tabs on dinner, while April took
a deep breath and went in search of Luca. Just as Tony
opened the front door she and Luca found each other.

He took her hand and kept her by his side. Why she
should be so nervous to meet his family made no sense.
Her only goal was to help him get his mother and grandmother to stop setting him up. Which meant she should
try to relax, listen carefully and follow Luca's lead. And
remember not to launch into one of her nervous run-
on sentences without taking a breath. She tended not
to censor her thoughts.

Luca's mother reminded April of her aunt Celia. Mrs. Paladino was at least five seven and wore her salt-and-pepper hair in a twist. She even had an oversize purse like Aunt Celia, who kept everything in it from Band-Aids to washcloths. Mrs. Paladino smiled politely at April, although her smile didn't reach her eyes. It was understandable. April was a stranger. It meant a lot that his mom was trying.

His father, on the other hand, grinned broadly as he offered her his hand. "April, yes?" he said. "No wonder Luca likes you. You're very pretty."

"Thank you, Mr. Paladino."

"I'm Joe. If you must, Joseph. That beautiful woman is my wife, Theresa. And here is my mother-in-law."

"It's lovely to meet you," the elder Mrs. Paladino said, grasping the tips of April's fingers in a perfunctory handshake.

"Call her Nonna," Joe said, although April had her doubts. Better not to call her by name at all.

"Is everyone here?" Theresa asked.

"Dom should be here any minute," Tony said. "Come into the living room. I'll pour drinks. Pop, you want iced tea?"

"No. I want Prosecco."

"Iced tea, coming up. Mom?"

"I'll also have the tea. And get Nonna her club soda."

April followed Luca's lead and sat next to him on the beautiful tan couch. "April," Theresa said as the drinks were doled out. "Luca tells us you're starting your own business."

"I will be, yes. It's a concierge service, one that will rely mostly on college students who've been carefully vetted to do everything from babysitting to food shopping to making personal deliveries."

Theresa nodded. Joe smiled. Luca squeezed .

"That sounds very modern," Joe said. "Some
for the Upper East Side."

"Yes, that's definitely one of my target markets. But
my research tells me that lots of people could use quali-
fied temporary assistants. After spending twelve hours
at work, it's nice to be able to have someone depend-
able to go to the market for you, or pick up the dog from
the groomers."

Joe nodded. "Very clever." He turned to his wife.
"That means you don't have to pay to keep someone
full-time. Smart."

"Theresa," Catherine said, coming in from the kitchen,
wiping her hands on her apron. "It's wonderful to see
you." She kissed Theresa's cheeks like a true European.
"I'm so sorry I wasn't able to greet you at the door. I was
tending the stove."

"It's all right, Catherine." Theresa looked her over,
but her smile was genuine. "I can smell your sauce
from here."

April expected a compliment, but none came. No
wonder Catherine was worried.

"I know it won't be as good as yours, but I hope you
enjoy it. Would you all like appetizers in here, or at the
dining room table?"

Tony stood. "Why don't we all move to the dining
room."

"May I help you serve?" April asked Catherine.

"That would be wonderful, thank you."

It was great to return to safer territory. The dinner would be several courses, from the *aperitivo* to the
digestivo, very traditional. April had only read about
meals like this.

By the time they'd set out the appetizers, Dom had

arrived, and April wasn't at all surprised to find he was devilishly handsome. Cut from the same cloth as his older brothers, who took after their father's side of the family. The smile he gave her was smooth, as was his handshake, and she could only imagine how much havoc he caused in the neighborhood.

He went over to Nonna next, and the way he teased her, sniffing her neck while she swatted at him, made April smile.

"Nonna, you're wearing new perfume. Do you have a date later?" Dom asked, still chasing the side of her neck. "I'd better meet him first, make sure he's a nice man."

"I'm not. *Smettila, pazzo.* Stop it, you crazy."

He kissed her loudly on the cheek. "I can't help it. You get more beautiful every day."

She scowled as her wrinkled cheeks got pink. But the moment Dom turned around, she smiled like a girl.

April liked him. He'd keep some lucky woman on her toes, that was for sure, but there was a natural warmth about him that all the Paladino brothers shared.

She took her place next to Luca, directly across from his mother. Of course, everything tasted delicious, and she was careful to compliment each dish but not too lavishly. By the time they reached the *secondo*, the meat and side dish course, April had relaxed, mostly because of how she'd been included in the easy conversations by almost everyone. The notable exception was Nonna, but April didn't take it personally. She was just grateful that Theresa hadn't given her the third degree.

But as she swallowed another bite of delicious zucchini fritter, the talk quieted, and she suddenly felt on edge, especially when Theresa looked at her expectantly.

Putting down her fork, April said, "I got a chance to look at some of Luca's custom furniture. You must all be so proud. I had no idea he was so talented. And, oh, gosh, the drawing for the new staircase that he designed for his apartment took my breath away. I couldn't help wondering if he'd worked on your living room, Catherine."

Shit. She'd obviously said something wrong. Everyone at the table was staring at her. Tony's fork had stalled halfway to his mouth.

After several uncomfortable seconds, Tony said, "Catherine had a designer, but she has remarkably good taste. Most everything you see is Catherine's doing."

April held back a whimper. She shouldn't have brought up Luca's custom work. He'd told her no one had seen the workshop. Stupid! And now she'd insulted Catherine, who'd been so nice to her.

She didn't look offended, though, and she gave April a reassuring smile.

Dominic coughed. She was pretty sure he was covering up a laugh.

"I've seen his work. It's not bad," Tony said with a teasing grin. "Seriously, the armoire you made for Eleanor Baker blew me away."

"Wait a minute." Catherine stared from Tony to Luca. "Why haven't I seen any of your pieces?"

Luca just smiled, but April could tell he wasn't pleased. He wasn't looking at her at all.

Until he did.

"I should have mentioned that we don't really talk about work at the dinner table. No big deal, though."

The WTF look Dom gave him told her that was a blatant lie.

Luca turned to his parents. "I don't think I mentioned to you that April has family in Positano. On her mother's side."

Had her mention of his custom woodwork been so out of line that he'd changed the conversation to that? She'd screwed up, and after all Luca had done for her. Even though she felt sick, it was all she could do not to guzzle the rest of her wine.

"It's beautiful in Positano," Catherine said. "Have you been?"

April smiled, determined to send her the biggest bouquet of thank-you flowers she could afford. "No, I've never been to Italy. My mother is second-generation Italian. She keeps in touch with our family there, so I'd love to go someday."

"What kind of furniture?" Joe asked, clearly puzzled and staring at Luca. "If you have time for a hobby, you should be starting your internship."

"Hey, Pop," Dom said, "you want more wine?" He stopped in midreach for the bottle. "Sorry, I meant to say iced tea."

Joe went off on how the doctors were trying to kill him. Everybody knew wine was healthy. The Paladinos in Naples all drank wine and half of them were older than Joe.

April glanced at Dom, who gave her a tiny wink. She was going to be bankrupt from all the flowers she was going to have to send.

"Tell April about the family, Pop," Tony said, and April breathed again.

Joe picked up the torch and proceeded to tell her the history of the Paladino family in Naples, while April did her best to continue to eat. Her stomach felt like lead, and all she wanted was to go back in time so she could keep her mouth shut.

Dinner went on, and everyone acted as though she hadn't been an idiot. Luca hadn't taken her hand again. But it could have been because he was using both his knife and fork.

This was supposed to have been a job. One she approached like any other. God knew she'd made the best of stressful situations before, but this was something different, even though it shouldn't have been.

She was glad to hear Theresa compliment Catherine on the meal. And no wonder. The dinner had been extraordinary. Everything about the evening, with one notable exception, had been perfect.

Everyone was very nice when it was time to leave. Even Theresa. Although she did ask about April's last name, and her eyebrows went up when she heard her father was a second-generation Dubliner. But honestly, what did it matter? April wasn't going to be joining their family. In fact, she had the feeling Luca would soon be telling his parents that they'd broken up.

Finally, she and Luca were alone together again. "I'm sorry about earlier," she said.

"What? About the furniture?" He waved down a cab. "Don't worry about it."

"I tend to get carried away. I should have thought—"

"Hey. It's okay."

"Yeah, well, at least it stopped your mother from booking the church, huh?"

He smiled. Kind of. It was crooked, and the way he looked at her made her realize she had no idea what he was thinking. Probably nothing good.

Thankfully, her cell phone vibrated in her pocket. She slipped it out just as the taxi pulled up, and there, big as life, was the one name she'd figured she'd never see again. *Wes.*

It took her a moment to catch her breath. She'd stopped leaving him voice mails a week ago and had pretty much ruled out the possibility of ever hearing from him again. Even her curiosity had dwindled. But if he wanted to return her money, even if only a portion of it, she was more than ready to listen. Just not at this moment. All she really cared about was making things right with Luca, so she slid the phone back in her pocket.

Luca put his hand on the cab door, but he didn't open it. "If you'd like to be alone to take that call, I don't mind walking home."

"No. It's fine. We can both take the taxi. I need to figure out what I'm going to say to him. All I want to do right now is scream at him for twenty minutes about what an asshole he is."

IF ANYONE WAS capable of screaming for twenty minutes, it was April. And Luca couldn't imagine anyone deserving it more than Wes. That first night she'd given it to Wes with both barrels, positively shaking with her anger. But as she sat looking out the window, her hands folded loosely in her lap, he wondered why she was so calm. Maybe it wasn't the first time he'd called. But if it wasn't, why wouldn't she have mentioned it to him?

He wasn't sure what to do. He wanted to ask what was going on, but she'd clearly decided not to say anything to him. It was her choice, of course, but it was strange. He felt as if he'd been a part of the whole Wes ordeal, although if he was honest, he had just been a bystander. Nothing about his relationship with April granted him rights to her private life. But he also knew she was smarting over the conversation at dinner. He didn't want to think he'd mishandled the situation, but he'd caused her to feel embarrassed. No excuse for that.

Then there was his dad's crack about not having time for a hobby. Thank God Dom had steered the conversation to another topic. Sometimes the kid surprised the hell out of him. The topic wasn't dead, though. Luca knew better than to believe that.

For once, the traffic wasn't too bad, but the awkward silence in the back of the cab made the trip feel longer. What Luca hated most was the damper the evening had put on his big surprise.

After paying the driver, Luca held open the cab door for April and scrambled for something to say. It wasn't until they got in the elevator that he gave up trying to be clever and just went for honesty. "Thank you," he said. "You were terrific tonight. I, on the other hand, didn't handle things well. I apologize."

Her eyes widened. "I'm the one who screwed up."

"No," he said, touching her arm. "You had no reason to think the topic was off-limits. It shouldn't have been. That's my own bullshit. I don't particularly like discussing my—" he snorted "—hobby."

"You heard Tony, he was impressed… Surely once the rest of your family sees how talented you are—"

"Look," he said, "my family expects me to get my architect license, and they have a right to expect it, not just because it's good for the business but because they think that's what I want. But just between you and me, I'm not sure I do."

April stared at him without saying a word, but questions flared in her eyes.

"It's not that I hate it, I'm just more interested in carpentry and working with my hands. But I don't want them to know that. So please don't say anything. You're the only person I've told. I never planned on telling anyone."

The elevator was taking forever. He would have to call the repairman to come check on it before the tenants complained.

"Of course I won't say a word. But frankly, I'm surprised you trust me at all."

Luca smiled. "That's the main reason I told you. I don't want you to feel bad about what happened or think it was your fault. My family's reaction had nothing to do with you. It was all me. You were great. From the minute we walked into the house."

"I'm really glad you told me, but honestly, they don't know what a skilled craftsman you are? You have a real gift, Luca."

The elevator stopped, and Luca wasn't sure why they were still talking about this. He wanted to put the whole subject to bed. And then put April to bed with him.

Once they'd entered the apartment, the way she looked up at him told him they hadn't finished the conversation.

"I just… Your family is so close and so warm, I find it hard to believe they wouldn't want you to be happy."

"I'm not unhappy. It means a lot to me to make my contribution to the family business. It's the right thing to do."

"Okay," she said. "I just hate that you're passing up the chance to work on something you're so passionate about." She studied him for a few seconds and then smiled. "I should warn you that once I'm rich enough to buy a house, you're the first person I'm calling."

He smiled back. "Good."

"So you'll give me a discount?"

"Absolutely."

He exhaled, glad that they'd regained their equilibrium. Although he wasn't sure how he felt about telling her the truth. In some respects it had been a relief. It would have been even better if he could have explained the Paladino Trust. Every one of the Paladinos had a duty to uphold the principles of the Trust, but every year the makeup of Little Italy changed and made it harder and harder to abide by all of its rules.

"So, Wes, huh?" he said, shifting to yet another uncomfortable topic.

Her expression plummeted. "Yeah. Wes."

"Is this the first time he's gotten in touch?"

She nodded. "I'm not sure what to make of it. I mean, it would be nice if he wanted to give me back the money he took, but I'm not holding my breath."

"You want to talk about it?"

She shook her head. "Not yet. I need to think. The last thing I want is to be caught off guard again. I think I'll be satisfied just to hear his reasons for being so shitty, but I don't know."

Luca nodded and started for his room. "I'm going to go change. But if you need someone to listen…"

She closed the gap between them and put her hand on his cheek. "Thank you. For being here, for confiding in me. Trusting me."

He kissed her, holding her arms, wanting much more than just this. But he also wanted this thing with Wes to be over. For all Luca knew, Wes might have all her money, and if that was true, who knew how long she'd stick around.

When they finally parted, he could see her hesitation, but she squared her shoulders. "I'm dying to get out of these heels," she said. "And to find out what that asshat wants."

Admiring her for once again facing the problem head-on, Luca watched her climb the stairs to her room. Even if Wes pissed her off, or disappointed her again, Luca still had that surprise up his sleeve. An affordable apartment ten minutes from his place would go a long way toward cheering her up. Or so he hoped.

17

BAREFOOT, IN HER most comfortable sweats and T-shirt, April sat cross-legged on the mattress and closed her eyes. She'd cleared her mind, putting aside the dinner, work, her desire for a chocolate bar and especially Luca so she could concentrate on what she wanted from Wes.

Of course she wanted her money. But she may only have one crack at talking to him and she wanted it to count.

He had to know that what he did was vile. That there was simply no excuse for leaving her in such a precarious, horrible position. Even if they'd only known each other for a day, his actions would have been despicable. So while laying out the precise ways she could verbally retaliate gave her a modicum of satisfaction, she was quite sure slinging missives at him would only put him on the defensive.

What did she know about Wes? That he was insecure, for one thing. While he'd been good at coding and was generally very tech savvy, he'd occasionally let slip how much he envied April's business sense and her ability to think quickly on her feet. And sometimes that made Wes feel small. Which wasn't her fault, but it might've played a part in his bailing out.

In retrospect, she hadn't really understood how immature Wes was.

Now that she'd gotten to see what kind of man Luca was, the difference between them was glaring. Wes was still a boy, even at twenty-six.

Thinking about Luca made her want to go downstairs and talk to him about the phone call, but she held back. This was her problem. One she had to figure out on her own. But after she'd finished talking to Wes? Knowing Luca would be there for her made everything easier.

She picked up her cell phone and took a deep breath. The likelihood of Wes returning all her money was slim. Did she want to get the police involved?

That option had been chasing around in her head for the past half hour. It wasn't something she could push aside and think about later. If she wanted to press charges, she'd have to watch her tone. Find out where he was staying.

The phone rang once. "April," he said, his voice tight. Nervous. "I didn't know if you would call back."

"Of course I would. I want my money."

"Whoa, okay. Straight to business, huh?"

"Jesus, Wes."

"No, no. You're right. I owe you an apology."

"Yes, you do. You also owe me several thousand dollars. My entire savings. Or has that slipped your mind?"

He sighed, and while she wanted to reach through the phone and grab him by the throat, she forced herself to calm down.

"I know I went about it the wrong way, but I didn't actually steal your money."

"And yet all the money I'd saved for the business vanished from the joint account."

"Well, yes, but—"

"You stole my money, Wes."

"Can we not use the word *steal*?"

April rubbed her eye. And she'd wanted to go into business with this idiot. "Go on."

"Okay. I didn't just take the money, I invested it."

"In what? A trip to Atlantic City with your college buddies?"

"No. Will you listen? Please? I invested it in a start-up. I knew the principles involved. I knew they had an outside source of funds and a heavy hitter ready to step in for 40 percent equity. It was a sure thing."

"Great, so you'll pay me back tomorrow? With interest?"

"Shit, April, come on. Give me a chance, huh?"

"I don't see any reason why I should. I take it the sure thing had a sudden, shocking setback?"

"Okay, yeah. But the money is still in play. And it's going to pay off, I swear. We can double our stake."

The money wasn't gone? She hadn't expected that. But it was still hard to hold back. She didn't give a damn about doubling anything, but she'd be a fool not to try to recover some of the money. Just so she could pay Luca back, if nothing else. "You had no right to do that without consulting me. Or to abandon me like you did. At the very least, you could have told me before I left St. Louis."

"I know," he said. "That's why I already bought a ticket to go back. I want to see you in person. Explain everything. Work out a way to make this right."

Make this right?

She was speechless at first. Speechless and embar-

rassed. How could she have fallen for a guy this stupid? He didn't even get that she would never trust him
again. He was a thief and a coward, who had left her at
a stranger's apartment with four squares of toilet paper.

"I'm not in St. Louis," she said, immediately regretting it. She should've let him make the trip for nothing, though she didn't want him talking to her parents.

"Where are you?"

"Unless you have my money, I have no desire to see
you." She was shocked at how calm she was being. His
stupid voice, his stupider excuses, hadn't sent her into
a screaming rage. But she needed to choose her words
more carefully. Let him have a little hope. Until he returned every penny.

"You're right," he said. "I did this all wrong. But I
swear to God I was trying to help. I thought we could
double our money and then we'd have some real juice
to start the business. I wanted to surprise you, April.
You'd done most of the work and I thought I could—
Look, this would be better in person. Are you still in
New York?"

"Yes," she said, not thrilled to tell him that much.

"You kept a little money aside, didn't you?" Wes
chuckled. "I knew if anyone could take care of herself,
it would be you. And look. Here you are, still in the city.
Where are you staying?"

As if her having the common sense to keep some
of her savings for an emergency was an excuse for his
behavior? God, maybe she should invite him over right
now so she could slap him until her hands were raw.
"It doesn't matter."

"Come on, April. I miss you."

She could only go so far with the *maybe I can for-*

give you act. It wasn't that she was afraid of the idiot, but she didn't want him to know where she was.

"I swear to God, April," Wes said. "I'll make good on this."

"I hope so," she said and left it at that.

After several long seconds of silence, Wes asked, "Are you still in Little Italy?"

April swallowed. "Call me when you have the money and we'll talk again."

She disconnected, knowing that wasn't the best way to end the conversation. Not if she wanted him to come through. But it was the best she could do.

She fell back, her head hitting the pillow, her arms fanning out to either side of the mattress. What a day. The stumble at dinner, the talk with Luca then Wes…

Now she really wanted a beer and to see Luca. But definitely not in that order.

Sadly, he wasn't downstairs, at least not where she could see him. She debated going to his bedroom, but since he had no door to knock on, it didn't seem right. Instead, she got a beer from the fridge and wrote it down in the little notebook that she kept by the microwave. Luca had teased her about keeping track of everything she used, but it was only fair. She grinned, thinking about the day she'd brought home bagels and he'd started his own page. Such a goofball.

She plopped down on his recliner and sighed as she visualized all her worries floating away. If she'd had the energy, she would have meditated properly, but at the moment beer and good thoughts were about as much as she could handle.

Footsteps came from the hall, and she couldn't help but smile, even though she didn't open her eyes. Until Luca lifted her whole body off the chair so he could

steal her seat. Which he instantly atoned for by settling her on his lap.

She wrapped her arms around him and let him kiss
her. There were few things in the whole world she liked
better. His hands were warm and gentle on her back,
and he seemed pleased when he realized she wasn't
wearing a bra.

"You," he said, pulling away just enough so they
could look at each other without going cross-eyed, "look
whipped. Gorgeous. Happy. But whipped."

"I am. Whipped, I mean. And happy. And I'm glad
you think I'm gorgeous."

His grin was like a balm to her soul. "How'd it go?"

"It was hard, especially when I had to be semi-nice
to him," she said, and Luca's brows shot up. "Well, if
you count refraining from cussing or yelling as being
nice. I have to be civil if I have any hope of getting my
money back."

"Okay."

"He's still a jerkface but the money isn't gone, or so
he claims. He says he invested it."

Luca's troubled frown deepened. "And you're okay
with that?"

"Hell, no." She smoothed the small crinkle between
his brows. "But honestly, I thought the money was long
gone. That I wouldn't recover a dime of it. But I'm willing to see how this plays out. Do you know how happy
it would make me to be able to pay you back?"

"Jesus, don't be nice to that asshat on my account."

April swept back the stubborn lock of hair that always gravitated to his forehead. "He was whiny and
apologetic. So it was fun letting him grovel."

Luca still looked awfully serious. "I don't care about
the money. I hope you know that."

"I care. I care a lot, and it bothers me."

His frustration was clear in the hard set of his jaw. "I wish you'd just forget about it."

She leaned back to stare at him. "Luca."

"I know. I'm sorry."

She hated the shift in mood, but she was glad he'd realized she wouldn't accept a free ride. "Aww," she said lightly, telling him all was forgiven. "Here I thought you came out here to try to get in my pants."

"Of course I'm trying to get in your pants," he said with a short laugh. "I also—"

She kissed him, just in case he was about to say something she wouldn't like, but then the kiss became more heated than she'd planned. When she had to breathe again, she whispered, "Lucky for you, I'm a sure thing."

He smiled and kissed the tip of her nose. "May I finish what I was about to say?"

"Only if it's something good."

"Tony found you an apartment not far from here."

April blinked. "Would you repeat that, please?"

Luca grinned. "It's a sublet, just a small one-bedroom. And get this, it's on Hester Street only a ten-minute walk from here."

"Wait a minute. This just happened?"

"Tony told me about it right before dinner. He knows the building manager and mentioned you were looking for a place. The guy who has the lease is working out of the country but doesn't want to let the place go because of the price deal."

April hadn't moved a muscle except to cross her fingers. "How much?"

"How does $450 a month sound?"

"Honest to God?" she whispered.

He nodded.

"Oh, my… When can I see it? Can we go there now? Is there a subway stop on Hester?"

Luca laughed. "Take a few breaths, okay?"

She tried to calm down but her heart, her pulse, everything was racing. If this turned out to be a dream she'd be so pissed. "When can I see it?"

"Monday afternoon. I'll get the key after work."

"Really? No sooner?" She bit her lip at her thoughtless ingratitude. "Monday will be great."

"There's some furniture the guy left, but I wouldn't get too excited about it."

Too late. She let out a happy shriek. "You know, I can pick up the key on Monday if that's easier."

"The management office is close to the job I'm working."

Once again, Luca had stepped up. He was her friend, her hero, her lover…

She threw her arms around his neck so he couldn't see the tears beginning to fill her eyes. "Thank you," she whispered.

APRIL HUGGED HIM so tight Luca felt like a million bucks. No ridiculous hours on the commuter train. No sleepless nights for him, worrying about her. She could work on getting her business going without having to sweat so much over money. Yeah, it would have been better if he could have told her the truth, but given that he wasn't able to explain the whole story, he felt damn good. He wanted her to flourish in New York. And it didn't hurt that they could see each other as often as they liked.

"How about your room tonight?" she asked as she pulled back. "Just for a change."

Luca grinned. "Good idea." He had the better mattress, so of course they'd been sleeping in his room exclusively. He was about to lift her up, but she slid off his lap.

"I have to run upstairs for a sec. I'll meet you in there, okay?"

"Sure," he said, noticing a trace of tears in her eyes. "Take your time."

After waiting until she was halfway up the stairs, Luca got up and grabbed a couple of water bottles. Happy as he was for her, he was going to miss having her at the apartment. The ridiculous office-slash-bedroom was still far too small to be of much use as anything but a home for the bed, but as soon as he remodeled upstairs they could have moved into his master suite. They would've both had plenty of room and closet space and...

Except it wasn't about that. April needed to know she could stand on her own.

April had beaten him to the room. She was taking off her clothes as he walked in, sending her T-shirt flying into the corner. His mouth watered at the sight of her breasts, jiggling softly as she stripped out of her sweats and panties. Damn, she was gorgeous.

"You going to stand there ogling me, or are you going to participate in this little party?"

His shirt was off before she had the covers pulled down, and everything else followed quickly, leaving him with an erection that needed tending. Every inch of her turned him on. Her knees, her shoulders. She'd cast a spell on him, and he wasn't complaining.

For some reason she was still standing at the end of the bed, which was too far away. So he climbed onto the mattress and crawled over to her. He wasn't sure why she was laughing. "What?" he asked, looking up.

"Nothing. Everything. You make me smile."

That wasn't what he'd been going for. He rose up on his knees, put his arm around her waist and held her steady as he nuzzled her neck, kissing her at the curve of her shoulder, leaving his mark behind. God, he hadn't done anything like that in years.

"Did you just give me a hickey?"

He leaned back, grinning.

She shook her head. "You're insane. But I like that in a man." She pushed him back using both hands, and he let her, falling sideways so he wouldn't break any parts as she climbed in next to him. Eventually, he stretched out, maneuvering his head to a pillow while April straddled his hips.

"Oh, really?"

She bit her lower lip and leaned over him while stretching out, her breasts a tantalizing inch away from his lips. He captured one ripe nipple between his teeth, making her jump. She didn't object, so he continued, using a mix of tongue and suction to make her squirm.

Her hands ended up on either side of his head, balancing herself while he switched to the other nipple. It was a bounty of riches, but when he pushed up with his hips, he found he wasn't angled the way he wanted to be.

He sucked harder while reaching down until his fingers brushed against her trimmed pubic hair. In this position, her lips were parted just enough for him to zero in on her swollen clit.

Her sharp intake of breath made his cock jerk, and he brought his free hand up so his fingers could tease her other breast, swirling around her pebbled nipple in sync with his tongue.

April hummed above him, rocking on her hands and

knees, forward and back, letting him play and explore. Making him burn with need.

He pulled back slightly and blew warm breath over her moist nipple. "You drive me crazy," he whispered.

She gasped. "What?"

"You," he said, moving his finger inside her, the warm, smooth wetness the most seductive sensation in the entire world, "make me crazy."

She arched her back and tried to kiss his mouth, but she couldn't reach him. "I want—"

Using two fingers, he thrust into her again. "What do you want?"

"You," she said. "Inside me."

"I am inside you."

"More," she whispered, then sat up, and he was able to look into her half-closed eyes. "Before…when I stretched…I was just getting this." She showed him the condom in her hand. Then she closed her eyes and squeezed the fingers inside her, and he nearly lost it.

"Gimme," he said.

"I'll do it. You just keep on…keeping on," she said, her words slurring slightly.

He loved that he could do that to her. Watching her slowly fall apart made him so hard he almost bucked her off with an inadvertent thrust. As she dealt with the packet, she continued to torment him. He groaned and twitched and it was all he could do not to come when she slipped the condom over his cock.

Her smile was pretty damn smug as she shifted just enough so that she could hold him steady as she lined him up.

"Oh, Christ," he said, the words slipping out of him as she lowered herself down inch by insane inch. The sounds he made after that were far too high to be his

voice, but shit, it felt better than anything was supposed to feel.

Jesus, he wasn't going to live through this.

When she hit bottom, they both stilled. Her grin was
slanted but happy. It was an amazing sight, looking up
at her, but he couldn't stand it. He reached for the back
of her neck and drew her down into a kiss.

When she pulled back, she didn't go far. He met her
gaze and didn't blink as he pushed up. They were close,
so close he breathed her breath. Her soft little whim-
pers got inside him as their connection grew and he
knew he'd never...

"I'm not going to last," he said. He stole another kiss,
but his head immediately dropped back onto the pillow.
He could feel the beginning of his orgasm. Slipping
his hand between them, he found her swollen clit and
rubbed her there. Seconds later she stilled, killing him
perfectly with the way she trembled and came.

That was all it took. To watch her eyes go dark,
her lips part on a silent cry, her body quivering in and
around him—he came so hard he was lost. And when he
found himself again, she was still in his arms. He helped
her lie down on her side, where they curled against each
other and relearned how to breathe.

APRIL DRIFTED ON the rise and fall of Luca's chest, his
strong arms keeping the rest of the world at bay. She
had no idea what time it was. The dark was broken by
diffuse light streaming through the new window shade,
and all she could hear was the beat of his heart, the
sound of her own sighs.

This was what she'd imagined when she'd pictured
herself in love.

Independence and support in equal measure. A man

who had nothing to prove. Someone who would make her want to be better, stronger. Kinder.

If only this was real.

And who knew? It could be. She still hadn't gotten past her luck over the apartment. How much more perfect could things have turned out? On the other hand, it wouldn't be easy sleeping on her own, in her own apartment, knowing Luca was just ten minutes away, sleeping alone. Or maybe he wouldn't be alone at all. With her gone, he could bring home dates again.

The thought turned her stomach.

She had to focus on the bigger picture. They wouldn't know if they had something lasting between them until she moved forward with her life, which included moving out. Thank goodness for her mentor, Elena, for the connections April continued to make. It would all come together; she knew it would.

Perhaps leaving the safety of Luca's arms would be her final trial by fire. She felt certain that no matter what happened between them, he'd always be there for her if she needed him. That was who he was.

She'd be there for him, as well. She hoped they would have another opportunity to talk about his future. He deserved to be happy in every aspect of his life. Surely there had to be a way he could help his family but still pursue his dreams?

Tonight, though, she would sleep in his bed. Listen to the steady rhythm of his heart. Soak in how lucky she was to have found the one man in all of New York who was perfect for her.

18

On Monday, April worked at a car show, handing out fliers. Although her feet were killing her at the end of the day, she'd made three hundred dollars. And in a couple of hours, she'd be able to see her new apartment.

By the time she walked through the front door, she had twenty minutes to change her clothes and shoes before Luca got home and they headed to Hester Street. She stopped in the kitchen and slipped the three hundred dollars into the envelope of cash Luca hadn't picked up from last week. It bothered her that he seemed to be ignoring it, but she'd already called his attention to it twice. After making a notation of the amount in her little notebook, she grabbed a bottle of water and took it upstairs with her.

When she heard Luca come home, she grinned. He couldn't see her and she couldn't actually see him. But the smile was automatic.

"Sweetheart?"

April heard his voice and froze. Had he brought someone home with him? Because he'd never called her that before. Nor had he used any other endearment.

"April?"

"I'm here," she said, her heart threatening to join her stomach.

She heard him run up the stairs, and then he was there. In her room. Putting his arms around her, pulling her close and kissing her.

"Hi," she said against his mouth.

"Hi, yourself."

"Are you alone?"

He leaned back and looked at her. "Yeah. Why?"

"Oh, no reason." She smiled big and moved closer. "Do you have the key?"

Luca smiled back. "Yes, but first I'm going to take a shower—"

"You don't need one. Honest. I'd tell you."

"I'll be less than ten minutes." He rubbed her back, long, slow strokes that made her knees weak, before he rested his hands on top of her butt. "After I finish kissing you."

Of course the kiss started heating up. In seconds he had his hand underneath her top, trying to find the clasp of her bra. His rock-hard erection had probably set a record.

She finally broke away just as he would've unfastened her bra. "Guess what?"

"What?" he said, clearly frustrated that she held him at arm's length.

"No shower. But you can change your shirt if you want, then we're going. But honestly even your shirt is fine."

He made a face.

"You wouldn't have started making out with me if you were too dirty."

Understanding registered on Luca's face. Laughing, he shook his head. "Fine."

THE APARTMENT WAS on the third floor of a four-story building. The elevator worked. The stairwells were clean and well lit, and the building had looked nice from the outside. There was a bus stop on the corner and a metro station a few blocks away. So far, so good. When she entered the third-floor hallway, it smelled fine, the paint looked fresh and the carpet looked older but clean.

"Here it is," Luca said, handing her the key to number 303.

She was almost afraid to open the door, but it couldn't be terrible, not if Tony thought it was decent. She turned the key, glad to see there was already a dead bolt lock. Walking inside, she hit the light switch.

It was love at first sight.

It was small, like every other apartment she'd seen in New York except for those belonging to members of the Paladino family. But it wasn't bathtub-in-the-kitchen small. There was a little red couch—okay, maybe a love seat—in the living room, which was sectioned off by a throw rug. The kitchen was basically one long counter that held the sink, the tiniest four-burner stove she'd ever seen and an apartment-sized fridge—and there was even space enough for her coffeemaker and microwave.

The linoleum floor had seen better days, but at least it wasn't cracked. The whole space had standard white walls, which was fine with her. There were two standing lamps and one light over the sink.

A long window was cranked open in the living room. The view was of a building across the way, but at least the area below wasn't filled with trash cans. No bad odors wafted into the apartment, and that was a blessing in the city.

"Luca," she said, turning to him. "Holy crap."

"Don't stop now. Keep looking." His arms folded over his chest, he looked so pleased he could pop.

"Right." The bathroom was really small. The toilet bore some faint rust stains, as did the small sink, but they were otherwise clean. The shower actually looked pretty decent. The water pressure sucked, but she wasn't about to complain.

Luca stepped aside so she could make the sharp right into the bedroom. There was a bed. With some linens on it. It looked to her like a full, but it could have been a queen. There was even a little closet that had empty hangers just waiting for her clothes.

"I'm sure we can find you a dresser and a nightstand at one of the resale shops in the neighborhood," Luca said. He peeked out the window on the far wall. "Ah, it's not even a busy street, you're lucky. You can see a tree from here."

She joined him, and finding his hand, she squeezed it. "Oh, my God. This is beyond my wildest dreams."

"It's pretty good," he said, "for New York."

"Big rooms are overrated. This is perfectly cozy. And I'll be able to put my stamp on it with some pictures and stuff. I bet I can fit a desk across from the couch, and a chair if I don't have a TV. It'll be great. I'll be able to work from here. Cook, so I don't have to get takeout all the time." She turned so she could look up into his eyes. "You think we ought to try the bed? Make sure we both fit?"

He nodded.

They didn't pull down the covers. Before she slept there, she'd go buy her own sheets and pillowcases.

"I'll ask my mom to send me some of my stuff," she said, as she lay down on the side of the bed nearest the door.

Luca joined her, and while it wasn't as roomy as his king, the mattress was comfortable, and it would work out fine. Better than fine. Because it would be hers. At least for a year. Who knew? Maybe Mr. DeLaria would stay in Rome forever, and she'd build her empire from apartment 303.

"That is one big smile," he said. "Tell me what you're thinking?"

"That I'm the luckiest person in the world. That I owe your brother a huge bottle of wine. I hope he likes cheap Chianti, because that's all I can afford, but I'll wrap it pretty. I'll have to find out about the Wi-Fi, though, but I'm not worried about it. And did you see the bus stop? It's so close."

He chuckled, his hands imitating hers, tucked under his chin. "I know. It's so great."

"But it is. It really is. This is the nicest place I've looked at by a whole lot."

He didn't even try not to laugh. "I'm so glad this makes you happy."

"It does. So much. And at this price? I'll totally be able to pay you back, with or without Wes returning my money."

"He'd better."

She shrugged. "We'll see. I don't want to think about him right now. I just want to sign all the papers immediately so no one can change their mind."

"I think you'll have to wait until tomorrow."

"I want to be there first thing."

"I'll make sure you are."

"I forgot to look in the fridge."

"I was assured everything was in working order."

"Still. I'll need to see it. And also, do you think that stove had an oven?"

"I think so. I'm sure it did. It was around twenty inches, and that's considered apartment-sized. But we can go take a look if you want."

"Not yet," she said, uncurling one of his hands so she could touch him. "It's going to be weird not coming home to your place."

"No one said you have to move right away. I mean, you could stay a few more days. Or maybe you should wait until you get that package from your mom. Have your own things when you're ready to move in."

April couldn't stop smiling. She supposed it was foolish to try to pretend she didn't love him. It wasn't just the apartment. Or any one thing. He was amazing in every way. Her real luck hadn't actually been finding this place. It was meeting Luca.

POOR LUCA. APRIL had kept him at the apartment far too long, until she finally realized he was starving. But instead of eating out, they decided to come back to his place and have food delivered. While he took the shower he'd wanted, she placed an order with their favorite Chinese place, then went downstairs to wait for the delivery guy while watching *Jeopardy*. Mostly, though, she daydreamed about how she'd fix up her new apartment.

When the doorbell rang, she had her cash ready, plus tip. But it wasn't Liu Wei with his usual smile. "Wes. What are you doing here?"

His blond hair was parted on the wrong side and slicked back with hair gel, otherwise he looked the same. And yet everything about him creeped her out. Especially his smile, which was wider than it had any right to be. "I thought I'd find you here."

"Doesn't mean you're welcome." She couldn't believe his nerve showing up like this. "Unless you have some money for me."

"I do."

"All of it?"

The smile dimmed. "Not quite. Can I come in?"

"I don't know," she said, studying him. She didn't recognize his clothes. He hadn't been a slick kind of guy back when they were together, but the suit he was wearing was just that. Slick. He probably thought he looked sharp, but the breast pocket of the jacket was slack, his white collar worn. The briefcase was new, though.

"Seriously?" he said. "At least give me a chance."

The sound of the water cut off. What if she let Wes in and Luca came downstairs wearing nothing but a towel? Not that she cared what Wes thought, but it wouldn't be fair to Luca. "You want me to trust you now, is that it?"

"Look, I feel like shit for what I did. And I've missed you. A lot."

She replied with an impatient snort.

"It's true. I honest to God thought I would surprise you by doubling the money we had. And then everything went to hell. But it's better now."

She heard Luca on the stairs, but she waited until he was almost at the bottom to turn. He wasn't in a towel, but in low-riding jeans and no shirt. Barefoot, hair wet and sexy as sin.

"That's really neither here nor there, is it?" she said, facing Wes again. This was Luca's apartment, but she knew he would be okay with whatever she wanted. "You know what? Come in. But you've got five minutes. That's it."

He crossed the threshold, but she didn't bother to shut the door or give him room to come any farther inside. If he did, he would see Luca standing by the stairs. If

Wes pissed her off, and the odds were high he would, she'd back him right out into the corridor.

Wes bent to open his briefcase and pulled out a folder. "If you just take a look at this prospectus for the start-up, you'll see why I was so impressed with it."

She took it and flipped through the pages. It certainly looked professional, but big deal. "Fine. I'll look through it when I have a chance." When hell froze over.

"It's a really solid—"

"Wes. Please."

He nodded, brought out two envelopes from the case, then closed it and stood. "Here's a thousand dollars," he said, handing her the first envelope. "I know it won't go far, but it's impossible to withdraw the funds at this point. It'll screw things up for everyone."

She closed her eyes. If he couldn't see what was wrong with that, he was hopeless.

"But I drew up an agreement. A payment plan." He handed her the second envelope. "It's worst-case scenario. If everything goes to hell, which it won't, I'll still pay you back."

"When?"

He sighed. "Come on, April. Let me buy you a drink and we can talk."

Behind her, she heard Luca approach.

Wes's eyes widened. "Paladino?"

Luca joined them at the open door. "I didn't think I'd ever see you again," he said, looking at Wes as if he was deciding which limb he was going to take apart first.

Wes's gaze darted to April. "What's going on?"

April opened her mouth, too stunned to speak. "What's going on?" she said finally. "Luca has been kind enough to let me stay here until I can find a place, which, I'm guessing you know, isn't so easy in this city. Especially when you don't have much money."

Wes looked at Luca again. April realized how close he was standing, which she didn't mind. Let Wes make any assumption he wanted.

"I knew you'd land on your feet one way or another," Wes said, narrowing his eyes. "I still worried you might be in a tight spot. But I can see that you're doing just fine."

"What are you inferring? That because I'm renting a room here, you're off the hook?"

The cynicism in his expression made her wince. It was his defensiveness, the need to rationalize the vile thing he'd done, of course. Some things never changed. "Hey, I can't blame you for finding a way to make life easier. Good for you. Smart. But then, you've always been clever. Used your assets well."

Anger shot through her and she felt her face heat with fury. "You need to leave. Now," she said. "I'll make any changes to the agreement I see fit and send you a copy and one to my attorney. Just so we're clear, I'm expecting payment in full. And soon, Wes. You stole from me and this agreement proves that you're culpable. Don't think for a minute I won't press charges if you renege."

"Oh, I don't doubt it. Hell, April, I was trying to make things right. You know what, though? It's actually a relief, finally seeing that you're not as perfect and self-reliant as you'd like everyone to believe." He snorted. "Here I'd wanted to show you I could carry my weight. I should have known."

Luca moved in. "She asked you to leave."

As if summoned, the elevator dinged. "Don't worry about it," Wes said, stepping back. "I'm gone."

She watched him leave, her stomach tight, her

thoughts spinning. So angry she wanted to scream. She had the sinking feeling that she could kiss the rest of her money goodbye. After what Wes had said, she couldn't seem to care that much. Ironic, since she needed to prove him wrong.

Luca touched her arm and she realized she was in the way. She moved back while he took care of the food delivery, her insides too twisted up for her to be interested in eating. She couldn't help wondering if there was more truth to what Wes had said than she'd like to believe. Sure, she was about to move into her own apartment, but that hadn't even been her own doing. She should've been out of there by now.

"Come on," Luca said, closing the door and taking her hand. "We're not going to let him ruin our evening."

No, she thought, they wouldn't. She'd already done that herself by overstaying her welcome.

"WHAT A DUMB BASTARD," Luca said, setting the take-out bag on the card table.

"I don't know what to say. Other than I can give you—" She looked at the envelope in her hand and held it out to him. "Here's a thousand dollars and I put three hundred in the envelope earlier," she said, glancing back at the counter where she kept that goddamn notebook. He swore he'd set a match to it. "Have you even calculated what I actually owe you? For incidentals, beer, everything? I might have enough or I can set up a—"

"Hey," Luca said. "Don't let the asshole rattle you. He was just trying to justify his actions, which are un-justifiable. Watch, he'll use this to try to weasel his way out of paying you back."

"Probably. I don't really have an attorney."

It took everything Luca had in him to smile. "I didn't think so." All he wanted to do was punch Wes.

"I should call Vinny. Get him to arrest that bastard. I don't know how much money makes it a felony, do you?"

Luca shook his head. "Stay away from Vinny. His dad and brothers are cops. That's the only reason he's wearing a uniform. He has such a lousy reputation with women he could make Wes look good."

April sighed. "So basically the only guys I attract are complete losers."

"Wait a minute," he said, waiting for her to say it was a joke. "What about me?"

"You?" She blinked. "It's different with you," she mumbled. "You didn't choose me. I barged into your life."

"Jesus. You're letting him mess with your head."

"I am not." She turned away to get the paper towels. "It's just the truth."

"Wait. Are you taking advantage of me?"

"No." Her gaze shot back to him. "Of course not. At least I don't mean to."

"Well, you're not. If I didn't want you here you'd be gone." He could see she was still upset. Her face hadn't lost its flush and she could hardly look at him. Gently, he lifted her chin so she would meet his gaze. "If you haven't noticed, I like having you here."

She studied with an intensity he hadn't seen before. "I want to believe that," she said, making him angry. "You can't deny I've inconvenienced you, though. Upstairs should've been done by now."

"Do you really think I give a shit about that? I'm glad to be in a position to help. As if you wouldn't do the same for me."

"I would," she said, "but—"

"No." He kissed her. Felt her trembling, for all the wrong reasons. He might still go punch out Wes. God-damn coward. "Remember, I came from my folks' house where it was noisy all the time. Believe me, you're a vast improvement."

That got her to smile. For a second at least.

DAMN, HE WISHED he could tell her the truth. That he didn't need the money. That he wanted her to stay. And not just because he was a nice guy giving her a break.

He wished he could explain the situation, make her understand why he could afford to be generous without revealing the Trust, but he couldn't do that. Besides, he knew she would think he was just being charitable, when the truth was so much more than that.

19

"WHAT DO YOU think of this one?"

Luca joined April as she slid open the drawers of a tall, slim cedar dresser. It wasn't as durable as hardwood, but for April's purposes it should serve her well. "It looks great," he said, pulling out his tape measure. He was on his lunch hour, shopping with April at Mrs. Brivio's resale shop.

After he'd checked out the dimensions, he nodded. "This would fit in your bedroom."

April ran her hand over the polished top. "I still can't believe the building manager didn't ask for a deposit. Otherwise, we'd be taking our search to the Goodwill."

"This will last a while," he said, already thinking it would be a simple job to build a nightstand to size and stain it the same color as the dresser.

"God, this is so exciting. I've only been in the apartment for a week and I've already found the perfect table and I'm pretty sure the chair from the flea market is going to work."

"Hey, listen," he said, stepping closer, getting a nice whiff of her perfume. She'd told him the name, but he just called it April's. If there weren't people here, he would've planted his nose against her neck by now.

"What?" she asked, giving him a gorgeous smile.

"I wouldn't mention the rent amount to Mrs. Brivio."

"I wasn't planning on it," she said. "I remember what you said about how everyone here likes to gossip. Not that I wouldn't mind hearing some, but I don't relish being the subject of it."

"Sorry. You're with me. People have seen us holding hands. It's far too late for anonymity."

"Well, at least I know everyone is more concerned about you than me."

"That's true."

"Oh, before I forget." She reached into her cross-body bag, so tiny it barely held a credit card and a cell phone. Ah, and her key to his place. She held it out to him.

"What's this?"

"I've moved all my things over to my apartment. I don't need it anymore."

"I beg to differ," he said, closing her hand around the key.

"You want me to keep it?"

"'Course I do. I want you to feel free to come over anytime," he said, feeling a tug in his chest. He hoped she understood nothing had changed between them.

"Really?" Her lips slowly lifted at the corners, and he welcomed her shy smile with relief.

"Yes, sweetheart." Screw the pair of older women eyeing them. Luca pulled April close and kissed her. "Really."

Her smile widened. "The manager gave me only one key. But we can stop at the scene of your youthful crime spree and make a duplicate."

"I never should have told you. You're gonna bring that up forever, huh?"

"Absolutely." She leaned over to kiss him then took a step to her right and waved at Mrs. Brivio, who had just emerged from the back room. "Mrs. B," she said. "I have an apartment!"

A WEEK LATER, after April had helped Luca with some painting, she convinced him to run an errand with her. "My God, that pot," she said, coming to a swift stop in front of Bowery Restaurant Supply. "I need that pot."

Luca backtracked to stand next to her in front of the large, chaotic store that was packed to the rafters with stuff of all kinds. "You mean the stockpot?"

She nodded. "It's perfect."

"It's bigger than your stove."

She sighed. "You're right. Back home, whenever we cooked it was always for an army. Plus, there were always people stopping by, and no one ever left the Branagan house hungry."

"Sounds a lot like my family."

She took his hand. "True," she said, sighing. "I'll never be able to have more than five people over."

"You know, my kitchen's going to be finished soon. You could cook there. Invite whoever we like."

"We?"

"I'd supply the wine."

"Would we have your family?"

"Sure. And you can invite your friends. I bet Grace would like to come."

"I'm sure she would." Turning to face him, she touched his cheek. "I'd be afraid to make Italian food."

"So, cook anything you want. Dazzle them with your culinary skills."

Grinning, April leaned into him. "Be careful. I haven't cooked for you yet."

"Speaking of which…I'm starving," he said, nuzzling her neck and whispering, "Guess what for."

"Poor you," she said, patting his hand. "First, I need to get my pots and pans and some silverware…"

"All right," he said, letting her drag him into the store.

She grinned, and she couldn't remember a better day. A better week.

His kiss, as always, made her swoon.

"ARE YOU COMING over tonight?" April asked.

He had her on Bluetooth as he worked, trying his hardest to finish her surprise nightstand before she had her friends over to see her apartment for the first time. "I'm not sure. Depends on how far I get on this… cabinet."

Her silence made him wince. He realized he should have just said he had to work late. It would be a lot easier for her to understand a remodeling deadline than him choosing a side job over her.

"So, you're at your workshop?" She tried to sound normal, but her tone confirmed he was right.

"Yep," he said, tempted to confess, but her housewarming party was coming up so fast, and he really wanted to surprise her. The nightstand would match perfectly with the dresser she'd bought from Mrs. Brivio. "Anyway, aren't you working an event tonight?"

"I am, but I should be done by 11:00 p.m."

She hadn't actually asked if that changed things, but he knew she expected an answer. The party had been a last-minute decision and he still had a lot of work to do on the nightstand. "I don't know, sweetheart. I wouldn't count on it. Besides, didn't you say you had a job early tomorrow morning? I don't want to be responsible for you being all grouchy because you didn't get enough sleep."

"But I haven't seen you in days."

"We had lunch together yesterday."

She paused, then with the exact same inflection said, "But I haven't seen you in nights."

"I know. And I hate it. I do. On the plus side, if I finish this project, I'll be able to spend the next two nights with you."

"I've got a really late event tomorrow. And then it's party day."

He let out a frustrated breath. If there was any way he would get out of there in time to spend the night with her, he would, but he had another surprise he had to tackle: a desk he'd already made but that required some fine tuning to work in her small space. The last thing he needed now was to rush things and get sloppy. "I miss you," he said. "A lot. But I don't know."

"I understand," she said, although he had a hard time believing she meant it. "Be careful, okay? I know you haven't had a lot of sleep."

"Neither have you. Get some rest and we'll talk tomorrow."

"Okay," she whispered. "Good night."

After he put his phone away, he turned back to his router, determined to make this his finest piece so far. She'd be happy once she knew it was all for her.

APRIL NEEDED TO get dressed. All she had to do tonight was pass out drinks for a couple of hours, then she could come back home and do just what Luca said. Get some much-needed rest.

Since she'd moved, her days had gotten even crazier. The business was taking up every spare minute that she wasn't working or with Luca. And it took a lot of effort to carve out time to see him. Not that she'd ever complain.

It had been clear when she moved it would be more difficult to be together, but she'd never imagined it would be this hard. They'd gone from sleeping together every night while she'd lived with him to five out of seven nights the first two weeks in her new apartment. And now it was more like three out of seven. What was next? Once a week? Gradually pulling away from each other like this had been her worst fear.

Determined not to let her mood spiral, she went to the bathroom to check her makeup then headed for the subway. Her timing was perfect, and after she found a seat the rocking of the train soothed her nerves. Three stops in, it occurred to her that she wasn't respecting Luca's passion for his woodworking enough. A man didn't become that skilled without putting in a tremendous amount of time and labor.

It was bad enough that his family dismissed it as a hobby. She wasn't about to do the same thing. Even if it took him away like it had tonight.

Still, maybe when she got off work, she would go to his place. Even if it just meant sleeping in the same bed together. The thought buoyed her spirits as the train rumbled along.

Okay. So even if this was the beginning of a new phase, a pretty sucky phase, it didn't mean the bloom was off the rose. Relationships took time and work. Her parents had taught her that.

She just hoped that Luca wanted it to work as badly as she did.

HER EVENT ENDED on time, for once, but the idea of taking the train home made her want to weep. She had changed her mind about surprising Luca by showing up at his place—he would probably still be at his workshop, anyway. She had to get over herself. He was busy. She was busy. They led busy lives, just like everyone else who worked in the city.

"Hey, you working tomorrow night's party, April?" Carly, one of the regulars, fell into step beside her.

"For that kind of money? Of course I'll be there."

Someone else from the mass exodus of event staffers—April couldn't tell who—gave a catcall whistle that would have pissed her off if it had been aimed at her. "What's that for?" she asked.

"Oh, my," Carly said as she looked over her shoulder.

Alison grinned. "Check out the dude coming up behind us."

April heard the bike before she saw it. When the Harley pulled up beside them, April's jaw dropped. Luca took off his helmet and shook out his hair. He was so gorgeous, she wanted to jump him right there. "What are you doing here?"

"I finished. Why don't you hop on? I'll take you home."

"I'm wearing the tiniest black dress ever made."

He leaned over and said, "Then you'll have to squeeze against me really tight."

She turned to stare down her coworkers. "Fair warning to whoever whistled," she said. "He's mine."

"Damn straight I am," Luca said, grabbing her around the waist and bringing her in for one hell of a kiss.

She supposed that meant that yeah, the rose was still in full bloom.

SATURDAY AFTERNOON LUCA arrived at April's apartment with the desk/nightstand combo about ten minutes before she was due home. They'd have about half an hour to get everything ready for the party, but he could tell from the scent of freshly baked cookies that she'd been busy preparing before her meeting. For a moment he debated leaving the pieces in the living room, but ended up taking them into her bedroom where they belonged.

Not five minutes later he heard April at the door. "Luca?"

"In here," he said, trying hard to keep his face neutral and let her find her gift.

"What is that gorgeous piece of furniture?" she asked as she entered the bedroom, a huge grin spreading across her face. "It matches the dresser perfectly. Seriously, what is this? I don't understand."

"Hold on a second," he said, laughing as she flapped her hands in her excitement. "I'll show you."

He took hold of the desk that lay almost flush against the top of the nightstand. It slid straight out toward him, on four castors. "It's a desk," he said, right before he turned the unit around, adjusted the height until it would fit over her bed and slid the base under her bed frame.

"It's a *desk*!" She turned from it to him. "It's like one of those hospital trays," she said. "But stunning. And oh, my God, please don't tell Mrs. B., but what you built makes the dresser look like painted particleboard. Oh, Luca, it's *perfect*."

She jumped up and he had to grab her waist while she put her arms around his neck. Her kisses covered his lips, his jaw, his cheeks, even his nose, and then she came back to his lips again. "Is this what you've been working on all this time?"

He nodded and her eyes welled with tears. Happy ones.

"Anybody home?" It was Dominic. Who was probably with Tony and Catherine.

"Sweetheart?" he said, hugging her a little tighter. "We have to get ready. Didn't you want to change?"

"Yes. I've got all the plates and stuff ready. And, uh, Patty's bringing a punch bowl and the sangria to go in it, so we'll need to make room on the table for that."

"I'll take care of it. You get dressed."

She kissed him again. "I'll thank you again later."

"Can't wait."

Feeling damn well pleased, he met his brothers and Catherine in the living room. She held an elegant cake platter, and Tony carried a cake box. Dom had brought a bottle of champagne. An expensive one.

"What was all that about?" Dom asked. "We heard loud voices."

"I gave April her housewarming present."

"Good for you, buddy, but weren't you cutting it a little close?"

Tony did them all a favor and gave Dom a punch in the arm. He just laughed, and Luca put everyone to work, setting out plates and napkins, then got the veggie platter out of her small fridge, along with a container of dip. Luca breathed in slow and easy, amazed at the contentment settling in his chest.

April made it back in the room just as the last two guests arrived. Luca had met Grace a couple of weeks ago, and he'd introduced himself to Patty as he took her punch bowl and the gallon container of cold sangria.

Trying to wrap her head around what still needed to be done for the party was turning out to be a tougher task than April had bargained for. She was still in shock over Luca's gift. It was the most beautiful and thoughtful present she'd ever received, and her heart was so full it was all she could do not to burst.

After hugs all around, she served drinks and made sure Luca's family had met her friends. Then she ushered everyone into the living room. It was a tight fit, but that was okay. "So, Alec and Jennifer couldn't make it, but I want to welcome all of you to my new home, one month to the day after I moved in." She grabbed Luca's hand and pulled him close. "But before we do anything else, you all have to come with me into the bedroom to see my present."

"Oh, here's my present." Grace handed her two tickets. "It's to an Off-Broadway play. And you don't have to take me if you don't want."

April stopped, grateful that Grace was becoming such a good friend. After pulling her into a hug, she said, "Thank you. Of course I'll take you."

"Okay, quit being so sappy and show us your boudoir," Grace said, smiling.

Grinning, April herded all six people into her bedroom. Dom managed to position himself shoulder to shoulder with Grace. Poor guy had looked gobsmacked from the moment he'd set eyes on her.

"This," April said, pointing to the desk-slash-nightstand, "is an original creation by the supremely talented Luca Paladino. Luca, could you please show them how it works?"

Clearly embarrassed by the attention, he demonstrated how to slide out the desk and use it with the bed.

"You made that?" Tony asked. "I don't think I've seen anything like it before."

Catherine ran her hand over the smooth wood. "Luca, this is stunning. I'm incredibly impressed by the craftsmanship. Tony, you never said he was this talented."

"Yeah, well…who knew?"

Dom just stared at Luca incredulously.

"Thanks, everyone, but why don't we all move back into the living room and get this party started."

As soon as the collective had relocated and piled their plates high with goodies, Luca got everyone's attention for a toast. Even Dom took a break from flirting with Grace to listen.

"I want to say congratulations to the remarkable April Branagan, who has worked miracles with this little apartment while getting quite a nice business off the ground. Personally, I don't know how she does it all, because every spare minute, she's working at an event or walking dogs, or recruiting talent or taking meetings. She's amazing. I have no doubt that she'll succeed in every endeavor she takes up. I'm just so grateful that she walked into my life."

Patty lifted her paper cup. "To April!"

April didn't even try to blink back her tears. Luca's arm slipped around her shoulder, and he gave her a squeeze. "It's true, you know," he whispered so that only she could hear. "You never cease to amaze me."

She held her breath, trying to freeze the moment, to remember every single detail before she turned to meet his gaze. "You are the best thing that's ever happened to me."

20

APRIL KNEW LUCA wasn't home yet, so she let herself into his apartment. It was going to be fun teasing him about how the elevator in *her* building was never out of order. She'd walked, carrying two big paper bags with her this time. She shouldn't have made them so heavy. It would take him months to miss the few things she'd borrowed for her party.

In the five weeks since she'd moved, what he'd accomplished at his apartment was amazing. The gorgeous staircase, with its dark hardwood steps and simple yet elegant wrought-iron railing, stole her breath every time she saw it.

He'd also finished installing the wood floors upstairs and reconfigured the master suite, which was now larger than her entire apartment. It still needed paint and crown molding and trim, but the bed was up there now.

Holding on to its position between the new kitchen and living room was the trusty old card table. Grinning, she set the bags on it, along with the folded paper that had been wedged underneath his door. She saw it was an estimate for the elevator repair addressed to the company that managed her building. Luca's name was

written on the outside. Odd. Luca wasn't responsible
for the elevator. And he didn't use a management company. He owned his apartment.

Leaving it on the table for him, she put a few things
away. And then couldn't help getting out a dust rag. He
kept the floors swept but he sure wasn't a fan of dusting.

Ten minutes later she heard the door open.

"Hey," she said, turning toward him.

"I was hoping you'd beat me home," he said, coming straight for her.

He looked so good. He always did, whether he was
wearing work clothes or chinos and button-down shirts.
Luca sent her pulse speeding every time she saw him.

He swept her into a kiss that was so desperate, they
might have been separated for a month instead of a
couple of days.

But then it was like that a lot of the time. When he
finally pulled back, the way he smiled at her made her
shiver. "How was your day?"

"Good," she said. "I did a roundtable practice session with my team at Entrepreneurs. They liked my
pitch. And my enthusiasm, although they thought I was
a little too perky."

"Too perky? You? No way," he said, laughing.

She grinned, saw the invoice on the table and handed
it to him before she grabbed the flatware she'd returned.
"I thought my building manager was a friend of Tony's.
I didn't realize you knew Francis, too. Or at least someone thinks you do."

When he didn't say anything, she turned to face him.
She'd never seen that expression on his face before and
it was suddenly so quiet one could have heard the pro-
verbial pin drop all the way in Queens.

"Luca?" she said, swallowing. The starkness in his eyes brought a lump to her throat. "What's wrong?"

He blinked and stared down at the invoice he'd fisted into a crumpled ball.

She moved closer and touched his arm. "You're scaring me. Please tell me what's going on."

He finally looked up. And this time she saw guilt. Regret. Fear.

Clearly, it all had something to do with the management company of her building. But what could it possibly— Was this about her miraculous apartment?

"Luca," she said, her voice barely making it out of her throat. "What did you do?"

His mouth worked for a second before the words came out. "Let me explain?"

The bottom fell out of her stomach. Her throat closed so tight she couldn't breathe. She didn't want to know. She could make it to the door in a few seconds, down the stairs in the blink of an eye. Instead, she made herself say, "Tell me."

His hesitation brought tears to her eyes, but she forbade them to fall.

LUCA HAD ALREADY blown it. Instead of thinking on his feet, he'd let his panic show, and there was no way out now. He wasn't allowed to tell her everything. But he also knew the next thing he said could spell the end of their relationship. "I might have had a small part in finding the apartment for you."

"Small part." April shook her head, her eyes dark as sorrow itself. "If it truly had been small, you would've told me then."

"I… Shit. I know Francis but I asked Tony to handle it because…" Christ, he could barely breathe. Her eyes were moving quickly back and forth, and he knew she was rewinding to that day, that fateful afternoon, how he'd sounded so innocent, how he'd lied so easily.

"Who owns my apartment?" She waited for him to respond, and when he didn't, she asked, "Do you?"

Fuck. "Not...exactly."

He shook his head, raging inside, trying to find an exit that wouldn't destroy everything. "I can't tell you. I would if I could, but it's not up to me."

"Oh, that's fine, then. That makes it all better. Treating me like I'm a child. Making decisions for me behind my back and lying. Pretending we actually had something. Yeah, why would I be upset about any of that?"

She leaned on the table, and for a moment he thought she might be sick. But she straightened. "Oh, God. I believed you," she whispered, staring at the far wall. "I convinced myself that you believed in me. What kind of a moron am I? I jumped in, what, twenty-four hours after Wes turned me into a joke?"

She looked at him again, her face flushed, her eyes blazing. "Telling me how strong I was. How independent. That was all bullshit, wasn't it? So what, you decided I was a convenient piece of ass you wanted to keep close by?"

"No. Jesus, April." Luca felt as if the dagger through his heart was real. "I did it because I care about you. So much. You'd had such rotten luck, and I didn't want you to get discouraged."

He stepped closer to her and she literally cringed.

It nearly killed him. "I wanted to give our relationship a chance."

April moved farther away from him, toward the door. "Our relationship? You don't even know me. I told you from the start I pay my own way, that I had faith in my business plan and I would stay the course no matter what."

"I know." His voice wavered. "I got too high-handed, but I was just trying to give you a leg up, that's all. You couldn't seem to catch a break. It was never my intention to undermine you in any way—"

"Why did you let me stay? The very first night?"

Luca tried to slow down his breathing. Stay calm. Make her understand. "Yeah, okay, I'm a nice guy. I couldn't throw you out. You were a stranger to the city and had been dealt a bad blow. And yes, I'll admit, it didn't hurt that you were hot, but believe me, I let you stay here after that because of who you are. If you'd been an ass, I would have kicked you out the next day."

He didn't dare move closer to her. She looked as if she was ready to bolt.

"Look, I'm nice, it's the way my parents raised me. But I'm not stupid. I got to know you. I saw how you handled crushing odds. I admired you. I still admire you, and all I wanted to do was to ease the way for you a little."

"A LITTLE?" APRIL WASN'T sure how much longer she could stay on her feet. "It's not even about that anymore. You can't tell me you admire me or how I handle setbacks and then turn around and *ease my way*. That tells me everything I need to know. You don't have any faith in me at all."

"Okay. Fine. You want the whole truth? It wasn't just kindness on my part. I was scared." His eyes closed. "No. Terrified. I didn't want you to go back to St. Louis."

"I told you that wasn't an option for me. That I knew I could make it here. But you didn't believe me, and that's the problem."

"Yeah, but you also told me your family does that. Everyone goes back home at some point. So at first I—"

"When they fail. Then they go back home. I won't fail. But you didn't think I had it in me to succeed."

"No, the problem isn't that I don't have faith in you. Hell, maybe I have too much," Luca said with a humorless laugh. "I knew if you decided the obstacles made the city a losing proposition, you'd take your new business elsewhere. St. Louis. Chicago. Wherever. You're smart. You'd do whatever it takes to succeed. I knew that." He shrugged. "Even if it meant you had to leave me behind."

April swallowed hard. He'd lost all the color in his face, and stupidly, the urge to make him feel better swelled inside her, but she pushed it down ruthlessly. How did she know the truth anymore?

He rubbed his face. "What's ironic? You have no idea how much I despised myself for kissing you that first night. I told myself it was a dick move. You had no place to live so I had all the power and you might feel pressured. What a joke."

"Please, God, don't make this my fault. I was very clear about the fact that I wasn't vulnerable. You knew that."

"Yeah, I did. And you were absolutely right. You weren't the one who was vulnerable," he said, his voice cracking on the word. "I was. And I've proved that by fucking up *everything*."

Turning enough to hide part of his face, he shrugged. "What the hell. I might as well come completely clean. Whatever you do, it's obviously your call, but—" He swept the hair off his forehead as she'd done so many times. "I love you."

For a long time she couldn't speak past her closed

throat. When she did, it sounded hollow. "If this were yesterday, I would have admitted I loved you, too." She paused to swallow and he started to turn back to her. "But in my...dream, you believed in me. And I could trust you."

Empty, she fled the apartment while her legs could still hold her.

21

"IF ANYONE ASKS me about April again, I swear to God, it'll be a year before I come to another family dinner."

Silence. Finally, Luca could breathe again.

Ignoring the stares and pitying looks, he poured himself more wine and looked out the patio door. He shouldn't have come. His family meant well but they'd end up pissing him off—or he'd end up pissing off one of them.

He and Dom were about ready to rip each other's heads off. Dom. Giving relationship advice. Whatever. Sure, he knew women. Could probably get laid every night, if he wanted. But beyond that? The kid didn't know crap. One day it was gonna bite him in the ass.

Thinking about that, Luca found a smile.

"I'm glad to see you still know how to smile," his mom said, coming to stand beside him.

"Mom, please."

"Yes. I'm your mother. I'm entitled to ask questions. Have you called her yet?"

"What? Since you asked me fifteen minutes ago?" He set down the glass. This was a mistake. He didn't want to hurt his mom's feelings, or his dad's. Mostly

he'd come to drop the bomb while they were all together.

He was going to tell them he didn't want to be an architect. He didn't want to waste two years of his life on
an internship. If having an architect on board at Paladino & Sons was that important, they could hire someone. Lord knew they had the money to do it.

Goddamn Paladino Trust. It had made them all rich.
And made them slaves at the same time. But he wouldn't
get into that this evening.

He'd just make his little announcement and leave.
They'd all understand, or they wouldn't. He'd blown
it with April but he wouldn't blow the gift she'd given
him. His passion, what he wanted to do with his life,
was worth more than filling a slot in the company's
plan.

"Mom." He looked into her worried face and gave
her a smile. "It's going to be okay. I promise. But I have
something to say." He turned to meet the eyes of his dad
and brothers. Nonna and Catherine, too.

They were his family, and they wanted what was best
for him. April was right. He'd lost sight of that.

He cleared his throat. "I'm turning down the internship," he began, and already felt five years younger.

THREE DAYS OF counting the hours, of no sleep, of making the hardest decision in her life, had inched by and
April was making tea. It was the only thing she could
keep down. The knock on the door startled her into
spilling the hot liquid on her hand.

She hadn't heard from Luca at all, and she hadn't
called him, either. She would, eventually, when she had
a few more days to gather her strength. But if it was
him at the door, fine, she wanted this over.

To say she was shocked to find Theresa Paladino standing there was an understatement.

"I'd like to come in," Theresa said.

Confused beyond words, April stood aside. Theresa looked over the small space then met April's gaze. "I'm here to talk," she said. "I know Luca is a grown man, and I'm interfering, but there are things you should know that he couldn't tell you. And I'm just sick of the Paladino Trust holding my sons hostage."

"Paladino Trust?"

"*In poche parole*—in a nutshell—the Trust was started in the early 1900s by Joe's ancestors. The first Paladinos who came to New York bought up much of Little Italy. A lot of the buildings here are owned by the family and that's why rents are cheap. The Trust is good—it helps people stay in the neighborhood, people who can't afford the crazy rents. But it's not the same anymore. Even the business is too bound by the agreements. One of which is no one can know. You understand? No one. Luca couldn't tell you."

After a moment of flailing, April asked, "So, why are you?"

Theresa clutched her bag tighter and straightened her back. "Because I love my boys and I want them to be happy. You made Luca happier than I've ever seen. You also made him brave. You know what he did?"

April shook her head, just realizing she hadn't even offered Mrs. Paladino a seat.

"He told his father and brothers to hire another architect if they want one. You helped him see that his real passion isn't to build chain stores. Why it's so hard for my sons to believe we want what's best for them, I don't understand. My boy loves you. He's miserable that he chased you away." She gave April another once-over, sniffed and said, "He could have done worse. And he says you can make lemon gnocchi."

April couldn't do anything but laugh. "I haven't spoken to him since we had our fight."

"How many times did I ask if he called?"

April bit her lip. Luca must've loved that. "You were nice to come here, Mrs. Paladino, but…I'm sorry. I've already decided. I'm leaving in two days," she said, feeling only slightly guilty for misleading the woman. April was moving in with Grace, not leaving New York. If that didn't pan out, she'd have to find another city to set up shop.

"So, you have two days. Think about it. Think about who he is, huh? You're a smart girl. He was foolish, but for the right reasons. Sometimes, that boy, he's just too honorable." Theresa reached over and touched the back of April's hand. "He doesn't know I'm here. And you can't tell anyone about the Trust, okay?"

Nodding, April felt dizzy and happy and sad all at once. Too honorable. Yes, she could see describing Luca that way. Before she'd even made sense of half of it, she heard the door close, leaving her alone with her thoughts.

Why hadn't Luca called? Probably because she'd been pretty harsh, but then what was she supposed to have thought? He really had made some bad decisions. *Because he'd been scared. Of losing her.* It was so hard to believe. A lot of what he'd said had been too difficult to accept. Until she'd had time to really think about it. Time to get over the anger and hurt, and remember who he was. Luca would never intentionally hurt her.

He was the best man April had ever known. Everything else aside, she'd never fit with anyone the way she did with Luca.

God, she missed him. So much. Maybe it was too late, but she got out her phone, anyway. He was still Speed Dial One. The phone rang four times then went to voice mail. "Luca. I've had some time to think, and I know I reacted badly to everything that happened but I was shocked…" Her voice broke and she disconnected.

Since he hadn't called before now, she already had her answer, didn't she? Shame hit her in waves. She could beg, point out that Wes had conditioned her to assume the worst about a man. But she wouldn't do that. She'd leave with some of her dignity intact.

But dammit, she didn't want to leave. They needed to talk.

A second knock on the door made her jump again. She opened it expecting Theresa.

It was Luca. With his phone out. "I was stuck in your elevator," he said. "I've never wanted anything more than to work this out. Never. I miss you. I love you. I love the way you think, your strength, your determination. I have a lot to explain, and I will. Every detail, if you'll let me. There's this Trust thing that's complicated, but you should know. Also, I've told my family I don't want to do my internship, and that's because of you. None of it matters, though, compared to how sorry I am that I caused you pain. That I let my fears overshadow what was good for you."

April smiled. He hadn't taken one breath during that whole monologue. She threw her arms around his neck and he picked her up and carried her inside.

"I love you, April Michela Branagan, and I want to spend the rest of my life showing you how much, if you'll let me."

She swallowed hard. Because he had to know. "I was scared, too. Scared I'd never see you again. Never be in your arms." He set her down and wiped a tear off her cheek. "I said hurtful things—"

"And I *did* hurtful things…" He cut off her protest with a fingertip on her lips. "The only thing I care about is hearing you say you love me. And that you have no doubt that *I believe in you*."

"I don't doubt you. I was hurt but I don't think I ever really thought you were playing me," she said. "Not you, Luca, never you."

"Hearing you say that means a lot." Emotion darkened his eyes. "I can't say it enough, but I've missed you so much." He held her a little tighter. "God, I love you."

"Me, too. I love you," she whispered, crying happy tears, until she could tell him just how much.

* * * * *

*Look for the final book in
the* NYC BACHELORS *miniseries!*

*SEDUCED IN THE CITY by Jo Leigh
is on sale April 2017, available online and at
your favorite bookstore from Harlequin Blaze.*

COMING NEXT MONTH FROM

HARLEQUIN®

Blaze®

Available January 17, 2017

#927 THE MIGHTY QUINNS: JAMIE

The Mighty Quinns • by Kate Hoffmann

Regan Macintosh is positive the stranger staying with her grandmother is a wolf in sheep's clothing. But when she comes face-to-face with the sexy Jamie Quinn, it's Regan who's in danger of being consumed—by desire.

#928 MR. DANGEROUSLY SEXY

The Dangerous Bachelors Club • by Stefanie London

When a stalker threatens his business partner and longtime temptation, Addison Cobalt, Logan Dane makes the case personal. But staying close to the irresistible Addison may be even more dangerous than Logan realizes...

#929 HER SEXY TEXAS COWBOY

Wild Wedding Nights • by Ali Olson

The attraction—and the hot sex—between maid of honor Renee Gainey and best man Jeremiah Richards is off the charts. But when the wedding is over, Renee isn't sure she can say goodbye to her Texas cowboy...

#930 IN HER BEST FRIEND'S BED

Friends With Benefits • by J. Margot Critch

When Abby Shaw and Trevor Jones met, the desire between them was left simmering because of their friendship. But when they finally cross that line, can they go back to just being friends?

YOU CAN FIND MORE INFORMATION ON UPCOMING HARLEQUIN® TITLES,
FREE EXCERPTS AND MORE AT WWW.HARLEQUIN.COM.

HBCNM0117

SPECIAL EXCERPT FROM

HARLEQUIN Blaze

Regan Macintosh doesn't trust Jamie Quinn's roguish charm, but her resolve to keep the sexy stranger away is starting to wane…and if she's not careful, their hungry passion could make them both lose control.

Read on for a sneak preview of
THE MIGHTY QUINNS: JAMIE,
the latest book in Kate Hoffmann's beloved series
THE MIGHTY QUINNS.

Regan walked out into the chilly night air. A shiver skittered down her spine, but she wasn't sure it was because of the cold or due to being in such close proximity to Jamie. Her footsteps echoed softly on the wood deck, and when she reached the railing, Regan spread her hands out on the rough wood and sighed.

She heard the door open behind her and she held her breath, counting his steps as he approached. She shivered again, but this time her teeth chattered.

A moment later she felt the warmth of his jacket surrounding her. He'd pulled his jacket open and he stood behind her, his arms wrapped around her chest, her back pressed against his warm body.

"Better?"

It was better. But it was also more frightening. And more exhilarating. And more confusing. And yet it seemed perfectly natural. "I should probably get to bed," Regan said. "I can't afford to fall asleep at work tomorrow."

He slowly turned her around in his arms until she faced him. His lips were dangerously close to hers, so close she could feel the warmth of his breath on her cheek.

"I know you still don't trust me, but you're attracted to me. I'm attracted to you, too. I want to kiss you," he whispered. "Why don't we just see where this goes?"

"I think that might be a mistake," she replied.

"Then I guess we'll leave it for another time," he said. "Good night, Regan." With that he turned and walked off the deck.

Her heart slammed in her chest and she realized how close she'd come to surrender. He was right; she was attracted to him. She had wanted to kiss him. She'd been thinking about it all night. But in the end common sense won out.

Regan slowly smiled. She was strong enough. She *could* control her emotions when he touched her. Though he still was dangerous, he was just an ordinary guy. And if she could call the shots, maybe she could let something happen between them.

Maybe he'd ask to kiss her again tomorrow. Maybe then she'd say yes.

Don't miss
THE MIGHTY QUINNS: JAMIE
by Kate Hoffmann, available in February 2017
wherever Harlequin® Blaze® books and ebooks are sold.

www.Harlequin.com